Vixen

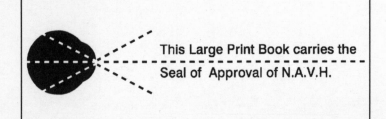

This Large Print Book carries the
Seal of Approval of N.A.V.H.

A NAMELESS DETECTIVE NOVEL

VIXEN

BILL PRONZINI

THORNDIKE PRESS

A part of Gale, Cengage Learning

GALE
CENGAGE Learning·

Farmington Hills, Mich • San Francisco • New York • Waterville, Maine
Meriden, Conn • Mason, Ohio • Chicago

GALE
CENGAGE Learning®

LIBRARY OF CONGRESS CATALOGING-IN-PUBLICATION DATA

Pronzini, Bill.
    Vixen : a nameless detective novel / Bill Pronzini. — Large print edition.
        pages cm. — (Thorndike Press large print mystery) (A nameless detective novel)
    ISBN 978-1-4104-8058-3 (hardback) — ISBN 1-4104-8058-5 (hardcover)
    1. Nameless Detective (Fictitious character)—Fiction. 2. Private investigators—California—San Francisco—Fiction. 3. Large type books.
I. Title.
PS3566.R67V59 2015b
813'.54—dc23   2015016777

Published in 2015 by arrangement with Tom Doherty Associates, LLC

Printed in Mexico
1 2 3 4 5 6 7 19 18 17 16 15

In memory of my grandfather
William Guder (1888–1958),
whose taste in reading matter
helped shape my own

PROLOGUE

Femme fatale. French for "deadly woman."

You hear the term a lot these days, usually in connection with noir fiction and film noir. Brigid O'Shaughnessy in *The Maltese Falcon.* Cora in *The Postman Always Rings Twice.* Phyllis Dietrichson in *Double Indemnity.* Matty Walker in *Body Heat.* Catherine Tramell in *Basic Instinct.* Scheming, sexually demanding vixens who trap their lovers in bonds of murderous desire and use them to further their own ends. Lethal women. Jezebel, Salome, Cleopatra.

But they're not just products of literature, film, the folklore of nearly every culture. They exist in modern society, too. The genuine femmes fatale you hear about now and then are every bit as evil as the fictional variety. Yet what sets them apart is that they're the failures, the ones who for one reason or another got caught. For every one of those, there must be several times as many who get away with their destructive crimes.

In the dozen years I spent in law enforcement and the thirtysome years I've been a private investigator, I never once had the misfortune to cross paths with this type of seductress. Never expected to. Never thought much about the breed except when confronted with one in a movie or the pages of a book or the pulp magazines I collect. Female monsters of a different variety, yes, like the middle-aged pair I'd encountered not long ago who made a living murdering elderly people for their money and possessions.

But a femme fatale in the classic mode? Not even close. If you'd told me that one day I would, and that her brand of evil would be like nothing I could ever have imagined, I would probably have laughed and said no way.

I'm not laughing now.

Neither is Jake Runyon. He was mixed up with her, too, in the same professional way I was, not quite from the beginning but even more deeply and all the way to the end. He'd never come across anyone like this particular vixen, either, and it left him as shaken as it did me.

Her name was Cory Beckett. Real name,

not an alias. A deadly woman who brought a couple of new twists to the species.

New — and terrible.

1

If it hadn't been for a bail bondsman named Abe Melikian, my involvement with Cory Beckett would have been peripheral instead of direct.

I was spending an average of only one day a week at the agency now. For one thing, I was not really needed. Business was steady, if not exactly booming — insurance and corporate investigations, mostly — and Tamara had the operation running smoothly in all phases. As far as the fieldwork went, Jake Runyon and Alex Chavez were able to handle most of it, and what excess there was went to part-time operatives. Runyon's relationship with graphic artist Bryn Darby and her young son seemed to be winding down; I inferred that from the facts that he was even more closemouthed than usual about his personal life and was again putting in long hours on the job, as he had before he'd met Bryn.

Another reason I spent less time at the agency was the promise I'd made to Kerry after once again almost getting my head shot off some months back: no more active participation in assignments that might put me in harm's way. The very personal investigation that had taken me to northern Nevada a short while ago — a plea from an old lover, Cheryl Rosmond Hatcher, whose son had been arrested for serial rape — hadn't seemed likely to involve any personal menace, though some had developed unexpectedly and unavoidably. If I'd known in advance that it would, I would not have gone. For that matter, once the trouble had been resolved, I was sorry that I had.

My promise to Kerry was one I had every intention of keeping. Her emotional state was still somewhat fragile after her kidnap ordeal in the Sierra foothills the previous July. Her recovery had been long and slow; it was weeks before she was able to shed the residual fear that prevented her from resuming normal activities, and there was no telling how long it would be before enough psychological scar tissue formed to seal off the wounds entirely.

During those first few weeks, she'd done all the work she was capable of for Bates and Carpenter by telephone and computer from the condo. She'd finally returned to her vice-president's office at the ad agency on a daily basis a little more than a month ago, and there'd been a noticeable easing of the strain that Kerry — and Emily, who had just turned fourteen, and I — had been under. Our home life was more or less stable again. Whatever else I did, I had to make sure it stayed that way by not burdening her with concern for my welfare. For that reason I had been careful to gloss over the hazardous incidents in Mineral Springs, Nevada.

With Kerry back at Bates and Carpenter and Emily in school, I had plenty of free time on my hands. But I was no longer chafing at semiretirement, as I had before those crazy few days in July. In this hyperelectronic age, most people seem unable to remain disconnected for more than a few minutes, as if they're afraid of being alone with their thoughts. Not me. I've always felt comfortable inside my own head. So mostly I filled up my days with househusband chores and shopping errands, reading and cataloging my collection of pulp magazines, doing other things I'd had little or no time for in the past — walks on the beach and in Golden Gate Park, museum visits, an occasional lunch and bull session with a few old friends and acquaintances. Come baseball season, I planned to attend as many Giants' afternoon home games at AT&T Park as I could. Work was no longer the be-all and end-all of my life, as it had been for so many years. Even an old dog like me could retrain himself if he had enough incentive — and if he could keep his paw in the game now and then, if only on routine cases.

A routine case was what I thought the Cory Beckett business would be when Abe Melikian laid it in my lap. I wasn't at the agency that day; I had been out to lunch with Ken Fujita, Intercoastal Insurance's claims adjustor, for whom I'd done some independent investigating in my lone wolf days, and I was on my way home when Tamara called my cell to tell me she'd just heard from Melikian. The case he had for us had something to do with a potential bail forfeiture, and he'd insisted that I be the one to discuss it with him and his — and our prospective — client. Would I be willing to meet with them at his office at three that afternoon?

Well, why not? I had nothing planned for the rest of the day, and Abe and I went way back. So I said yes.

Big mistake.

The client was Cory Beckett.

■ ■ ■ ■

I had no real inkling of her true nature at that first meeting. My initial impression, in fact, was that she was not the sort of woman who was likely to need the services of a private investigator. In her late twenties — twenty-eight, I found out later. Strikingly attractive, her sex appeal the low-key, smoldering variety. Sitting demurely in Melikian's private office, dressed in an obviously expensive caramel-colored suit and a high-necked, green silk blouse. The outfit, and the filigreed gold and ruby ring on her little finger, indicated she was well fixed financially — always a plus in a prospective client.

She had long, thick, wavy black hair and a model's willowy, long-legged figure, and wore a worried smile that even tuned down had a good deal of candlepower. But what you noticed first, and remembered most vividly, was her luminous gray-green eyes. They had a powerful magnetic quality; I could feel the pull of them, like being drawn into dark, calm water. It was only when you got to know who and what she was that you realized the calm surface was a lie, that underneath there weren't only smoldering sexual fires but riptides and whirlpools and hungry darting things with razor-sharp teeth.

Melikian did most of the talking at first. He was one of the more successful bondsmen in the city, with half a dozen employees and offices across Bryant Street from the Hall of Justice — a big, gruff second-generation Armenian noted for being a chronic complainer and poor-mouth, as well as for his shrewd business acumen. I'd done a fair amount of work for him over the years, to our mutual satisfaction and trust, which I supposed was the reason he'd insisted on dealing with me personally. He hated bail jumpers, as he called them, even more than other bondsmen did; to hear him tell it, they were all part of a vast conspiracy to ruin his business and drive him into bankruptcy. As a result he was careful to avoid posting bond for anyone who struck him as a potential flight risk, but now and then he got burned anyway. Usually when that happened, he ranted and raved and threatened dire consequences. Not this time. When I sat down with him and Cory Beckett, he was meek as a mouse.

She was the reason. Those eyes and that sleek body of hers had worked their spell on him; he hung on her every word, and the gleam in his eyes when he looked at her was neither cynical nor professional. An even more telling measure of how she'd affected him was an unprecedented willingness to split the agency's fees with her if I accepted the case.

The subject under discussion was Cory Beckett's brother, Kenneth, who had been arrested and arraigned six weeks ago on a grand theft charge. The bail amount was a cool fifty thousand, which meant she'd had to put up the usual 10 percent commission in cash plus some kind of collateral for most or all of the rest. I didn't ask what the collateral was; it was none of my concern.

"The trial's three weeks off yet," Melikian said, "so we got that long to save the bond and the kid's tail. But technically he's already a jumper on account of one of the terms the judge set for his bail."

"Which is?" I asked.

"Not allowed to leave the city without police permission. The court finds out he's in violation, the judge'll issue a bench warrant for his arrest."

"Uh-huh. And he's already gone."

"Yeah. And it don't look like he's coming back for his trial, unless you find him and get him back here in time."

"Does his lawyer know he skipped?"

"Sam Wasserman? Hell, no. And he won't find out if we can help it."

That was easy enough to understand. Wasserman was a well-respected criminal attorney, but something of a straight arrow in a profession sprinkled with crooked bows. If he knew his client had skipped, he would probably inform the court and then withdraw from the case.

"How long has your brother been gone, Ms. Beckett?" I asked her.

"At least three days," she said. She had one of those soft, caressing voices, maybe natural, maybe affected. Intimate even when she was playing the worried little sister.

"At least?"

"I had some business out of the city and when I returned, he was gone from the apartment we share."

"What did he take with him?"

"Clothing, a few personal belongings."

"Cell phone?"

"Yes, but he has it turned off. I've left a dozen messages."

"Why do you think he ran away? At this particular time, I mean."

"The strain must have gotten to him. . . . I shouldn't have left him alone. He's not a strong person and he's terrified of being locked up for a crime he didn't commit."

With any other client, Melikian would have rolled his eyes at that. Nine out of every ten bonds he posted was for an innocent party, to hear them and whoever arranged their bail tell it.

I said, "You have no idea where he might have gone?"

"None. Except that it won't be far, and he'll either be at a yacht harbor or marina — some kind of boat place — or there'll be one close by."

"Why do you say that?"

"Kenny hates traveling alone, any kind of long-distance travel. He won't fly and he's never driven more than a hundred miles in any direction by himself. And boats . . . well, they're his entire life."

"Working on or around them, you mean?"

"That's what he does — deckhand, maintenance man, any job that involves boats."

"Has he ever been in trouble with the law before?"

"No. Never."

So the self-imposed travel restrictions didn't necessarily apply. Fear of being sent to prison can prod a man into doing any number of things he'd shied away from before.

"The grand theft charge," I said. "What is

19

it he's alleged to have stolen?"

"A diamond necklace. But he didn't steal it. I *know* he didn't."

That meant nothing, either. Most people refuse to believe a close relative capable of committing a serious crime, no matter how much evidence exists to the contrary.

"How much is the necklace worth?"

"Assessed at twenty K," Melikian said.

Some piece of jewelry. I asked who the owner was.

"Margaret Vorhees."

"Vorhees. Related to Andrew Vorhees?"

"His wife," Cory Beckett said. "His drunken, lying wife."

Andrew Vorhees was a relatively big fish in the not-so-small San Francisco pond. High-powered leader of the City Maintenance Workers Union, yachtsman, twice unsuccessful candidate for supervisor. A man with an underground reputation for fast living and double-dealing and a penchant for scandal. It was whispered around that he had kinky sexual tastes, had been a regular customer of one of the city's high-profile madams whose extensive call-girl operation the cops had busted a couple of years back. It was also whispered that his socialite wife was a severe alcoholic. She had cause, if the rumors about her husband were true.

"How does your brother know Margaret Vorhees?" I asked.

"He doesn't, not really. He works . . . worked for her husband."

"In what capacity?"

"Caring for his yacht. At the St. Francis Yacht Harbor."

"Is that where the theft occurred?"

"She claimed it was, yes — the Vorhees woman. From her purse while she was on the yacht."

"Why would she have a twenty-thousand-dollar necklace in her purse?"

"Taking it to a jeweler to have the clasp repaired, she claimed. My brother was the only other person on board at the time."

"Where was the necklace found?"

Cory Beckett sighed, flicked a lock of the midnight hair off her forehead. "Hidden inside Kenny's van."

I didn't say anything.

"He swears he didn't steal it," she said, "that he has no idea how it got into his van. Of course I believe him. He's not a thief. He had no possible reason to take that necklace."

"Except for the fact that it's worth twenty thousand dollars."

"Not to Kenny. He doesn't care about money. And he certainly wouldn't have

21

taken it to give to me, as Margaret Vorhees claims. Or any other woman. No, she put the necklace in his van, or had somebody do it for her."

"Why would she want to frame your brother?"

"I don't know. Neither does he. Some imagined slight, I suppose. Rich alcoholics . . . well, I'm sure you know how erratic and unpredictable people like that can be."

"Is your brother the kind of man who makes passes at married women?"

"My God, no. What kind of question is that?"

"Sorry, but it's the kind I have to ask."

"Kenny's not like that at all. He's a very shy person, especially around women. He's never even had a girlfriend. His only real flaw . . . well . . ."

"Yes, Ms. Beckett?"

She ran the tip of her tongue back and forth across her lips, moistening them. The movement made Melikian squirm a little in his chair. "If I tell you," she said, "you'll think he's guilty, that he stole the necklace because of it."

"My job is to find him, not judge him."

". . . All right. It's drugs."

"What kind of drugs?"

"Amphetamines."

"How bad is his habit?"

"It's not a habit, really. He only uses them when he's stressed out. But they don't help, they just make him paranoid, even delusional sometimes."

"Violent?"

"No. Oh, no. Never."

"Do you know who his supplier is?"

"No idea. I don't take drugs."

I hadn't even hinted that she did. That kind of quick defensive response is sometimes an indication of guilt, but it was none of my business if she snorted coke five times a day and had a Baggie of the stuff in her purse. No judgments applied to her as well as her brother at that point.

I said, "How much money did he take with him, do you know?"

"It couldn't be much more than a hundred dollars. Wherever he's gone, he'll try to get some kind of work connected with boats. That's the way he is, no matter how much money he has."

"Does he have access to any of your bank accounts?"

"No. We keep our finances separate."

"Credit cards?"

"I let him use mine now and then, but . . . no, none of his own."

"You said he drives a van. Make, model, color?"

"A Dodge Ram, dark blue. The right rear panel has a dent and a long scrape — a parking lot accident."

"Can you give me the license number?"

She could, and I wrote it down.

"Anything else you can tell me that might help me find him? Friends in the area, someone he might turn to for help?"

"There's no one like that. He doesn't make friends easily." Cory Beckett shifted position in the chair, recrossed her legs the other way. Gnawed on her lip a little before she said, "Do you honestly think you can find him?"

"Sure he can," Melikian said. "He's the best, him and his people."

She said, "I don't care what you have to do or what it costs."

Abe winced at that, but he didn't say anything.

"No guarantees, of course," I said. "But if you're right that your brother is still somewhere in this general area and working around boats, the chances are reasonably good."

"The one thing I ask," she said, "is that you let me know the minute you locate him. Don't try to talk him into coming back,

24

don't talk to him at all if it can be avoided. Let me do it — I'm the only one he'll listen to."

"Fair enough. You understand, though, that if he refuses to return voluntarily, there's nothing we can do to force him."

Melikian said, "She understands. I explained it to her."

"And that if he does refuse, we're bound to report his whereabouts to the authorities."

Cory Beckett nodded, and Abe said, "Do it myself, in that case," without looking at her. He wouldn't sacrifice even a small portion of fifty thousand to keep his own mother out of jail.

"One more question," I said. "If we find him and bring him back, how do you intend to keep him from running away again?"

"You needn't concern yourself with that. I guarantee he won't miss the trial." She added, not so reassuringly given the fact that he'd already skipped on her, "Kenny and I are very close."

I asked her for a photograph of her brother, and she produced a five-by-seven color snapshot from a big leather purse: Kenneth Beckett standing alone in front of a sleek oceangoing yacht. You could tell he and Cory were siblings — same black hair, though his was lank; same facial bone structure and wiry build — but where she was somebody you'd notice in a crowd, he was the polar opposite. Presentable enough, but there was nothing memorable about him. Just a kid in his early twenties, like thousands of others. The kind of individual you could spend an afternoon with, and five minutes after parting you'd have already forgotten what he looked like.

We got the paperwork out of the way, and Cory Beckett wrote me a check for her half of the retainer; we'd bill Melikian for his half. The check had her address and phone number on it. The apartment she shared with her brother was on Nob Hill, a very expensive neighborhood. Melikian had mentioned at the start of our conversation that she worked as a model. One of the more successful variety, apparently.

We shook hands — hers lingered in mine a little too long, I thought — and she favored me with another of her concerned little smiles while Melikian patted her shoulder and chewed on her with his eyes. And that was that. Routine interview. Routine if slightly unusual skip-trace. Nothing special at all, except that for a change the client was a piece of eye candy.

Just goes to show how wrong first impressions can be.

2

From Bryant Street I drove to the agency offices in South Park. It was almost five by then, but Tamara, a workaholic like Jake Runyon was and I used to be, would probably stay until seven or so. Unless she had a date tonight. She'd taken up again with her old boyfriend, Horace Fields, who had moved back to the city from Philadelphia after losing both his cellist's chair with the philharmonic there and the wife he'd dumped Tamara for. The reconciliation was a mistake, as far as I was concerned — she didn't seem as happy as she should have been if it was working out well — but she hadn't asked for my opinion and I hadn't offered it. The Dear Abby syndrome is not one of my shortcomings.

I gave her a capsule report on the interview, then put the notes I'd made in order and gave them to her to transcribe into a casefile. Tamara does most of the agency's computer work — I've learned to operate one of the things, but with limited skills and a certain reluctance — and she is about as expert as they come. She also co-ordinates the various investigations, handles the billing and financial matters. Tamara Corbin, twenty-eight-year-old desk jockey dynamo who had tripled our business since I'd made the wise, very wise, decision to make her a full partner.

She set to work on the preliminaries. Skip-traces are an essential part of the agency's business, along with insurance-related investigations and employee and personal background checks, and most can be dealt with by relying on the various real-time and other search engines we subscribe to. The Beckett case didn't seem to be one of those because of the circumstances and particulars, but you never know what might turn up on an Internet search.

She suggested I hang around while she ran the initial checks — she's fast as well as expert — and I did that. Kerry wouldn't be home much before seven and Emily would get dinner started; singing was her primary passion, but she also loved to cook. Very good at both, too.

I was in my office, going over the file on a new, and routine, employee background check, when Tamara came in through the open connecting door carrying a printout in one purple-nailed hand. The purple polish didn't go very well with her dark brown skin, or at least I didn't think it did, but I wouldn't say anything to her about that, either. Who was I to criticize the fashion trends of a woman young enough to be my granddaughter?

"Nothing much on Kenneth Beckett," she said. "No record prior to the grand theft charge, just a couple of minor moving violations and a bunch of parking tickets, most of them in the L.A. area. Worked at two yacht harbors down there, Marina del Rey and Newport Beach. Good employment records in both places, left both jobs voluntarily for unspecified reasons. Worked on Andrew Vorhees' yacht for six months before his arrest — no problems there, either. Parents both dead, no family except for the sister. No traceable contacts with anybody else down south or up here."

"Pretty much confirms what Cory Beckett told me about him."

"Yeah. But I'll bet she didn't tell you anything about *her* background." Tamara waggled an eyebrow. "Juicy stuff."

"What, you checking up on our clients now?"

"After that fiasco with Verity Daniels, you bet I am."

The Daniels tangle was a sore subject with me, too. It had landed Jake Runyon in jail on a bogus attempted rape charge, almost gotten the agency sued for malfeasance, and its finish was the source of my promise to Kerry to keep myself out of harm's way.

"Besides," Tamara went on, "her background and her brother's are pretty closely linked. Kenny may be a nerd, but she's anything but. Some real interesting facts here."

"Such as?"

"For one, she's not a model. Not now, not ever."

"No? Then what does she do for a living?"

"Marries rich dudes. Two of 'em so far."

Well, that wasn't much of a surprise. "Married now? She wasn't wearing a wedding ring."

"Nope. First husband divorced her after eight months. She got enough of a settlement to set her up real sweet for a while. Number two, rich dude named Lassiter, lasted a little over a year. No divorce there, though."

"No?"

"Guy offed himself."

"For what reason?"

"Financial setbacks, according to the note he left," Tamara said. "But there's more to it than that. Two grown sons from a previous marriage claimed Cory was responsible for Lassiter's suicide."

"On what grounds?"

"Several. Two substantiated affairs during the year of marriage. Quote, bizarre sexual practices detrimental to his mental health, unquote."

"Bizarre in what way?"

"Not a matter of public record. Could be anything from orgies to goats to whips and chains."

"Goats?"

Tamara chuckled. One of her less-than-endearing traits is an off-the-wall sense of humor that she sometimes uses to shock my old-fashioned sensibilities. "Sons also claimed she mishandled finances, and coerced their father into making a new will that cut them out of the estate and left everything to her. They sued and had enough legal chops to get a favorable ruling. They got the big slice, she got a little one. Case brought her some negative publicity — probably one of the reasons she moved up here."

"So she's a promiscuous gold digger. What does that have to do with her missing brother?"

"Nothing, maybe. Except that both her exes owned yachts berthed at local marinas, the first one in Marina del Rey, the second in Newport Beach — the same places Kenny worked."

I chewed on that for a bit. "So maybe it was the husbands who got him his jobs there."

"Uh-uh. He was working at both marinas before she hooked up with either guy."

"Well? Maybe she likes boats, too, hangs around where her brother works, and that's how she met the future husbands."

"Or Kenny set up the meetings for her."

"What're you suggesting? The two of them working a scam to find her eligible marriage partners?"

"Could be. He trolls around, finds a likely prospect, baits the hook, and she does the rest."

"Immoral, if so, but not illegal."

"No, but if that's the game, neither one of 'em's as innocent as she pretended to you."

"Clients have lied to us before," I said. "We don't have to like them or believe them as long as the lies have no bearing on the job we're hired to do. You know that. Besides, Abe Melikian's footing half the bill, and we know he's all right."

Tamara said cynically, "Good thing for him he's not a rich yachtsman," and retreated into her office.

Since the Beckett case was essentially mine, I was back at the agency again the next morning for the follow-through. Tamara had compiled a list of all the yacht harbors and marinas in the greater Bay Area — quite a few, large and small, within a seventy-five-mile radius — and she and I called the ones large enough to have full-time staff members who could check their records for recent hires. No Kenneth Beckett or anyone answering his description at any of them. Finding him wasn't going to be that easy. If he was working at all, it could be for a private party rather than as an employee of a marina, boatyard, or boat owner. Or at a marina or boatyard outside the seventy-five-mile radius. And in any event, he might well be using a name other than his own. It would take legwork, possibly a lot of it, to track him down.

In the old days I handled most of the field jobs myself, until it got to be too much effort for even a fairly robust man in his sixties. Now and then I make an exception and climb back into the field harness, but hunting for Kenneth Beckett wouldn't be one of those times. Likely the search would require piling up a considerable number of highway miles, showing Beckett's photograph and asking the same questions over and over again — pretty dull and time-consuming work.

Not for Jake Runyon, though. He thrived on that kind of assignment. Liked being out on the road, moving from place to place. Worked best when he could set his own schedule, his own pace. And there was enough gap time in his caseload to allow him to take on the Beckett hunt.

Good man, Jake, a former Seattle cop and former investigator for one of the larger private agencies in the Pacific Northwest. Big, slab-faced, hammer-jawed. Smart, tough, loyal, and honest as they come. He'd moved to San Francisco after the cancer death of his second wife, to try to reestablish a bond with an estranged gay son from his first marriage, the only family he had left. The restoration attempt hadn't worked out; he and Joshua were still estranged and would likely remain so.

Runyon had been something of a reticent loner, still grieving for his dead wife, the first year or so he was with us. He'd come out of his shell somewhat after his hookup with Bryn Darby, but now that the relationship might be ending, he'd begun to drift back into his loner mode. A hard man to get close to in any case. My connection with him was mainly professional; we didn't socialize, probably never would. But we got along well, and more importantly, we had each other's backs. I'd trust him in any crisis and with my life — had done both, in fact, on more than one occasion.

Tamara and I were just finishing up when Runyon stopped in to deliver some material he'd dug up on a consumer fraud case. We briefed him on the Beckett investigation, and after he'd looked over the casefile he asked, "Priority job?"

"Medium to start," I said. "Beckett's trial is three weeks off, but it might take a while to find him."

"Okay. I'll get moving on it right away."

3

JAKE RUNYON

It looked like a fairly routine case to him, too, at first. He'd handled dozens like it over the years — skip-traces, bail jumpers, missing persons — and with less information than he had to go on here. Assuming the sister was right about Kenneth Beckett's habit patterns, the odds were pretty good that he could be found before the trial date. Beckett didn't seem to be either mature or bright, which made him a poor candidate for grounding himself without leaving a trackable trail. The one potentially tricky part, once he was located, was convincing him to come back to the city to stand trial.

There were more than two hundred marinas and boatyards on Tamara's list. But Runyon figured he could eliminate the ones in close proximity to the city — Oakland, Alameda, Sausalito, Pacifica, the near end of the Peninsula. Even a half-smart, short-tether runaway who didn't like to travel would choose a hiding place at some distance from his home turf. The remaining possibilities within a seventy-five-mile radius could be covered by one man in the allotted time frame, though if Runyon couldn't get a line on the subject in a week or so, Tamara had said she'd assign Alex Chavez or part-timer Deron Stewart to help out.

Runyon started in Half Moon Bay, moved from there to the mid-Peninsula area, then down to San Jose and the rest of the South Bay. No luck.

Stockton, Antioch, Rio Vista, Martinez, Suisun City, Vallejo. No luck.

The North Bay next, beginning with Sausalito, even though it was just across the Golden Gate Bridge, because of the town's large number of boating facilities. Another blank there.

And one more in San Rafael.

On up to Port Sonoma. And that was where, on the morning of the fifth day, he finally got his fix on the subject's whereabouts.

The Port Sonoma marina was located in a wetlands area along the Petaluma River near where it emptied into San Pablo Bay. Good-sized place with a ferry landing, a fuel dock and pump-out station, bait shop on one of the floats, and several rows of boat slips. The craft berthed in the slips were all sailboats and small inboards — no big yachts.

The day, a Saturday, was warmish for late November, and the marina was doing a moderately brisk business — individuals and groups getting their craft ready to join those that already dotted the bay and the winding upland course of the river. Runyon went first to the bait shop, but nobody there recognized the photo of Kenneth Beckett. Same at the fuel dock. He walked down through an open gate to the slips. The first half-dozen people he buttonholed had nothing to tell him; the seventh, a lean, sun-bleached man in his mid-fifties working on the deck of a Sea Ray Sundancer, was the one who did.

The boat owner took a long look at the photo before he said, "Yeah, I've seen this kid. How come you're looking for him? He do something he shouldn't have?"

"Yes, and he'll be in more trouble if I don't locate him soon. When did you see him?"

"Last weekend. No, Friday, actually — week ago yesterday."

"Here?"

"Right. Looking for work, he said. Seemed

to know boats pretty well. But nobody's hiring, so I told him to check up at Belardi's."

"Where's that?"

"Upriver six or seven miles."

"What kind of place?"

"Wide spot on the river — sandwich and bait shop, a few slips, some old fishing shacks. I heard the owner, old man Belardi, was looking for a handyman to fix up the rundown pier they got there."

"How do I get to Belardi's by car?"

"Easily. Go east on the highway, turn left at the first stoplight — Lakeville Highway. Six or seven miles, like I said. Can't miss their sign."

Belardi's turned out to be one of those little enclaves that look as though they've been bypassed by time and progress. The restaurant and bait shop, the pier and sagging boathouse, the handful of slips, the scattering of small houses and even smaller fishing shacks nearby all had a weathered, colorless look, like buildings in a black-and-white fifties movie. The Petaluma River — a saltwater estuary, Runyon had heard somewhere, that had been granted river status so federal funds could be used to keep it dredged for boat traffic — was a couple of hundred yards wide at this point, its far shore a long, wide stretch of tule marsh threaded with narrow waterways. More tule grass choked the muddy shoreline on this side.

Several cars were parked in the gravel lot in front, none of them a dark blue Dodge van. Runyon crossed past the restaurant to a set of rickety stairs that led down to another gravel area, this one used as a combination boat repair and storage yard. From the stairs he could see that some recent work had been done on the short, shaky-looking pier that extended out to the slips. Two men were on board an old sportfisherman, one of five boats moored there; another man was just climbing up onto the pier from the float between the slips. None was Kenneth Beckett.

Runyon braced the man on the pier first, got a couple of negative grunts for the effort. The two on the sportfisherman didn't recognize the subject's photo, either, but one of them said, "Talk to old man Belardi inside. Maybe he can help you."

Old man Belardi was an overweight seventy or so, cheerful until Runyon showed him the snapshot; then his round face turned mournful. "Don't tell me you're a cop."

Runyon said, "Private investigator," and

41

proved it with the photostat of his license.

"Well, crap," Belardi said lugubriously. "I get somebody I can rely on, hard worker, don't give me no trouble, and now you're gonna tell me he's a thief or molester or some damn thing."

"You did hire him, then?"

"Yeah, I hired him. Minimum wage and a place to stay. Seemed like a good kid, hard worker like I said —"

"A place to stay. Where?"

"Here. One of the river shacks."

"Which one?"

"Last to the north."

"He there now, would you know?"

"If his van's there, he's there. I don't pay him to work weekends. Plenty of business, good weather like this, and the customers don't want to put up with noisy repair work."

Runyon nodded his thanks and started away.

"Hold on a minute," Belardi said. "What you gonna do? Haul the kid off to jail or something? Leave me with nobody to finish his work?"

"He'll be going back to the city, one way or another."

"I'm too old to make those repairs myself and a regular handyman costs too much. I don't suppose you could hold off a few days, let him get the hard part of it done?"

"No. Not possible."

Belardi sighed. "No damn luck, me or the kid."

A paved driveway led downhill to the boatyard, and a rutted, weed-choked track from there along the river to where the shacks squatted on the marshy ground. They were small, board-and-batten structures of one large or maybe two small rooms that must have been there for half a century or more; a short, stubby dock leaned out into the muddy water in front of each. There was no sign of life at the first two. The third also appeared deserted until Runyon rolled up in front; then he could see the van pulled in close to its far side wall — Dodge Ram, dark blue, with a dented rear panel.

The sister's instructions were to notify her as soon as Kenneth Beckett was found, without contact with the subject, but Runyon was too thorough a professional to act prematurely. He'd make sure Beckett was here and would stay put before reporting in.

He pulled up at an angle so the nose of his Ford blocked the van, got out into a stiff breeze that carried the briny scent of the river and marshland. A long motionless row of blackbirds sat on a power line stretched across the hundred yards of open land between Lakeville Highway and the river, like a still from the Hitchcock movie. Somewhere upriver, an approaching powerboat laid a faint whine on the silence.

Runyon followed a tramped-down path through the grass to the shack's door. A series of knocks brought no response. He tried the knob, found it unlocked. Pushed on it until it opened far enough, creaking a little, to give him a clear look inside.

Half of the riverfront wall was a curtainless sliding-glass door; it let in enough light so that he could make out a table, two chairs, a standing cabinet, a countertop with a hotplate on it, and a cot pushed in against the side wall. Kenneth Beckett lay prone on the cot, unmoving under a blanket, one cheek turned toward the door and draped with lank black hair half again as long as it had been when the snapshot was taken. The one visible eye was shut. No sound came out of him.

From the doorway Runyon couldn't tell if he was asleep or unconscious. Or even if he was breathing.

4

JAKE RUNYON

He went inside. The interior was full of odors — dampness, mustiness, stale food, soiled clothing. None too tidy, either: empty cans of pork and beans and beef stew, empty milk cartons, unwashed glasses, plates, utensils in the sink and on the drainboard. Beckett, on his own without supervision, seemed to care little about cleaning up after himself.

Runyon leaned over the motionless figure on the cot. The kid was breathing, all right, in a fluttery kind of way — stoned, maybe. There was no visible evidence of drugs or drug paraphernalia in the room, but that didn't mean there was none hidden away somewhere.

Leave him be, make his call? What he should've done, probably, but instinct dictated otherwise. He gripped Beckett's shoulder and shook him, kept shaking him until the kid moaned and tried to pull away. Runyon put both hands on him then, turned him over on his back. That woke him up.

He stared up at Runyon through pale blue eyes that took several seconds to focus and then filled with scare. He said thickly, "Who're you? I don't know you. . . ."

"My name is Runyon, Jake Runyon. I'm here to help you."

"Help me? I don't need any help. . . ."

Beckett struggled to sit up. Runyon let him do that, but held him with a tight hand on his shoulder when he tried to lift himself off the cot. The left side of his face began a spasmodic twitching.

"You high on something, Ken? Amphetamines?"

"What? No! I don't use drugs."

"It won't do you any good to lie to me."

"I'm not lying. I've never used —" Beckett's head jerked suddenly, as if he'd been touched by a live wire. His mouth bent into a transverse line. "Oh, Jesus! She told you that, didn't she? *She* sent you!"

"If you mean your sister —"

"Another one, a *new* one."

"You're not making sense —"

Without warning Beckett lunged upward, tearing loose from Runyon's grip, thrust a shoulder into him, and streaked for the

46

door. There was surprising strength in the kid's wiry body; the contact sent Runyon reeling sideways into the table, barking his shin against one of the wooden legs and almost taking him off his feet. By the time he recovered, Beckett was through the door.

Runyon hobbled out after him, spotted him running for his van. Beckett pulled up when he saw the Ford blocking escape. He stood poised indecisively for a couple of seconds, then lunged past the van at an angle toward the river's edge.

The tide was on ebb and the bank mostly mud and sparse patches of grass. Beckett lurched and slogged along it to where an old rowboat was drawn up, caught hold of the stern and tried to shove it into the water. But it was mired deep in the brown ooze; he couldn't break the mud's hold. Runyon was almost on him by then. Beckett threw a panicky look over his shoulder, tried again to run. This time he got no more than ten feet before his feet slid out from under him and he went down in a sideways sprawl.

When Runyon reached him, the kid was dragging himself onto his knees. He hauled him upright and spun him around. He had forty pounds on the kid, plus his years of judo training when he was on the Seattle PD; he was prepared to use force if Beckett tried to knee or kick him. But that didn't happen. Struggled some, that was all.

Runyon said sharply, "Quit it! Stand still! You're not going anywhere until we talk."

The squirming stopped. Beckett stood with his eyes downcast, his breath coming in short, quick pants. Streaks of mud made the right side of his face look like he'd put on half of a brown mask.

"I don't want to talk to you."

"You're going to whether you like it or not. Back inside. Come on, no argument."

Beckett gave him none on the slog back to the shack, but he held tight to the kid's arm to make sure. He shut the door behind them and walked Beckett to the cot, sat him down on it again.

"You calm enough now to listen to me?"

"Why can't she leave me alone?" Beckett muttered. "Why can't everybody just leave me alone?"

"Listen, I said. I'm not involved with your sister; I've never even met her. I'm a private investigator — the agency I work for was hired to find you. You understand?"

"Investigator?" It seemed to take a few seconds before the meaning of the word computed. "You mean . . . Cory hired you?"

"Her and your bail bondsman."

Beckett drew a long, shuddery breath.

48

Then he pushed up off the cot again, but he wasn't trying to run this time. "Thirsty," he said, and groped his way to the sink, ran water into a milk-scummed glass, gulped it down.

"Better wash some of that mud off while you're at it," Runyon said.

The kid did as he was told, splashing water, scrubbing with both hands. He didn't make much of a job of it; he was still smeared with brown streaks when he finished. He toweled off and came back to sit on the cot again with his chin lowered, not making eye contact.

"I won't go to prison for something I didn't do," he said. "Not for Cory, not for anybody."

"If you don't show up for your trial, you'll go to prison whether you're innocent or not. You've already violated the terms of your bail."

"You can't make me go back."

"That's right," Runyon said. "But if you don't return voluntarily, I'm required by law to report the violation and the judge'll issue an arrest warrant. Is that what you want?"

Beckett stared off into space, eyes bright with misery. After a time he said thickly, "None of this'd be happening if Cory

49

hadn't talked me into it."

"Into what?"

Headshake. Runyon repeated the question twice more before he got a low-voiced response.

"Taking the blame."

"The blame. For the crime you're charged with?"

"Pretending it was me she was out to get."

"She? Who are you talking about?"

"Mrs. Vorhees."

Runyon backed away from the cot, swung one of the chairs away from the table and straddled it. "Let's get this straight. Did you steal Margaret Vorhees' necklace?"

"No. Nobody stole it."

"Then how did it get into your van?"

"Chaleen put it there. She told him to."

"Mrs. Vorhees did?"

"No, no. Cory."

"Why would your sister do that to you?"

Headshake.

Runyon asked, "Who's Chaleen?"

"That bastard. She's letting him do it to her, too."

Trying to make sense of what Beckett was saying was like riding on a fast-moving carousel. Round and round, round and round, and not getting anywhere. "Where did Chaleen get the necklace?"

"From Mrs. Vorhees. She wanted him to hide it in Cory's car so it'd look like she stole it."

"How could Cory be blamed if you were the only other person on the boat that day?"

"I wasn't. She was there when Mrs. Vorhees showed up."

"To see you, you mean?"

"No. Mr. Vorhees. She . . . No, I'm not supposed to talk about that."

"Talk about what?"

Headshake.

"Who told you not to talk? Cory?"

Headshake.

"All right," Runyon said. "So your sister was the intended target, but she talked this Chaleen character into framing you instead. Is that what you're saying?"

"Yeah. She can make anybody do anything she wants. Anybody. Anything. Any time."

"Why would Mrs. Vorhees want to frame your sister?"

"She hates Cory."

"Why?"

Headshake.

"When did Cory tell you you had to take the blame? Before or after Chaleen planted the necklace in your van?"

"Before."

"And you just let it happen?"

". . . I told you, she always gets what she wants."

"That doesn't answer my question."

"She said we had to, we couldn't rock the boat."

"What boat?"

Beckett said in a mimicking falsetto, " 'Trust me, Kenny. I know what's best for both of us. You won't go to prison, I promise.' " He seemed close to tears now. "She doesn't care about me. She says she does, but she doesn't, not anymore. She never cared about anybody but herself. It's all that goddamn Hutchinson's fault. . . ."

"Hutchinson. Who's he?"

Headshake.

Ramblings. Yet as improbable and inconsistent as Beckett's story sounded, it didn't strike Runyon as lies, delusions, or drug-induced fantasy. The kid was an emotional weakling strung out on fear, not a chemical substance. Fear of his sister, it seemed, as much as of being sent to prison.

"Anything more you want to tell me, Ken?"

"No. I shouldn't have . . . I . . . no."

"So what's it going to be? Back to San Francisco voluntarily, or do I notify the authorities?"

A rapid series of headshakes this time. "I

want to stay here," he said. "I like it here."

"You can't do that. I told you, it's either your apartment or a jail cell on an unlawful flight charge. Be smart. Let me take you back."

"No."

"Then let your sister come and get you —"

"No!"

"I have to tell her as well as the authorities where you are."

Beckett flattened himself facedown on the cot again, yanked the blanket up to his neck. "No more talking . . . my head hurts, I can't think. Go away, leave me alone."

"Listen to me —"

"No! Go away!" Another upward jerk on the blanket so that it covered his head. Burying himself under it. Hiding. "Go away, go away, *go away*!"

Runyon had no choice now. He went outside to call the agency.

5

I seldom go into the office on Saturdays anymore; it was pure chance that I happened to be at my desk when Runyon's call came in. My weekends are usually reserved for family activities, but this day was an exception.

Emily was one of the leads in a musical production her school was putting on and had to attend a semifinal rehearsal, and Kerry had gone over to Redwood Village, the Marin County care facility where her mother, Cybil, lived. Cybil is eighty-eight and in fragile health, not quite bedridden but no longer able to get around much by herself. The three of us had visited her the previous Sunday, but Kerry was worried about her and wanted to see her again, even though they talked on the phone nearly every day now. I offered to go along, but she said no, too many visitors at once was too tiring for Cybil and she would rather just make it a mother-daughter visit this time.

That was fine with me, but it left me at loose ends. I did not have anything I particularly wanted to do by myself, didn't feel like spending the day alone at the condo. There was some paperwork to be finished up on the employee background check, so I decided I might as well go on down to South Park. I had company while I slogged through the notes and printouts on my desk because Tamara had decided to work today, too, as she often did on Saturdays. She was even more of a workaholic than I'd been in my prime.

She was busy at her computer, so I took Runyon's call. Good news that he'd found Kenneth Beckett, but the details of their conversation didn't set any better with me than they did with him. Jake's instincts are pretty well honed; if he believed Beckett's story was straight goods, then it probably was. Which, as Tamara had suggested, made Cory Beckett the complete opposite of the person she'd pretended to be in Abe Melikian's office. Control freak, sex addict, schemer. With motives that didn't seem to make much sense. Why would she talk her brother into taking the fall on a bogus theft charge? How could it benefit either of them?

I'd told Tamara that it didn't matter if a client lied to us as long as it had no effect on the job we'd been hired to do, and that was true enough up to a point. But if the lies and misrepresentations involved a felony, we had a legal obligation not to ignore them.

"You haven't notified the client?" I asked Runyon.

"No. I thought I'd give Beckett a few minutes to calm down, then make one more try at reasoning with him."

"Likely to do any good?"

"I doubt it. He's pretty strung out."

"But not on drugs."

"No. Doesn't look to be any in the shack, but I'll search it after we're done to make sure."

"So that's probably another lie by his sister. She didn't want us talking to him, but in case we did we'd put down anything he said to junkie ravings."

"Same take here."

"Okay," I said. "Suppose I break the news to her, see if I can find out what she's up to. If you can convince Beckett to let you bring him back, go ahead. But in that event deliver him here to the office for the time being, not to their apartment."

"Right."

"Let me know if that's how it plays out. Otherwise, hang around the shack and keep an eye on him until you hear from me."

"He's not going anywhere," Runyon said. "I've got his van blocked with my car and his keys in my pocket to make sure."

After we rang off, I went in to brief Tamara. She said, "Weird. What d'you think the Beckett woman's up to?"

"No idea . . . yet."

"How about I do a deep backgrounder on her? That stuff I pulled up last week only scratched the surface."

"Go ahead when you have the time."

"Like right now."

The Beckett apartment on Nob Hill was only ten minutes or so from South Park, but street parking up there is always at a premium and garage parking fees are exorbitant. It took me another ten minutes to find curb space, one that was only marginally legal and two steep uphill blocks away.

I was short of breath by the time I reached the building, a venerable four-story pile near Huntington Park that may or may not have been some fat cat's private mansion a hundred years ago. Nob Hill, or Snob Hill as the locals sometimes call it, is where many of the city's upper-class families and affluent yuppie transplants hang their hats. It takes big bucks to live there, and I found myself wondering if Cory Beckett had dragged enough out of her two marriages to pay the rent, or if somebody else — not her deckhand brother — was contributing to the monthly nut.

Right. Somebody named Andrew Vorhees.

In the coincidental and serendipitous way things sometimes happen, I had probable confirmation much sooner than I could have expected. About ten seconds after I reached the building, as a matter of fact.

Just as I stepped into the vestibule, the entrance door opened and a lean guy with tanned, craggy features came striding out. His glance at me as he passed by was brief and dismissive; I was nobody he knew. But I'd seen his picture and I knew him: Andrew Vorhees in the flesh.

I managed to catch the pneumatic door just before it latched, slipped inside as Vorhees turned out of the vestibule. He had to have been visiting Cory Beckett; that he knew one of the other tenants would be stretching coincidence to the breaking point. It was possible the visit had something to do with his former employee and the theft charge, but more likely his reasons were the same personal ones that had brought her to his yacht the day of the alleged theft. Nice conquest for a scheming woman, if they were lovers — a man in the same wealthy yachtsman class as her two ex-husbands. The fact that he was married wouldn't mean much to a playboy with his reputation, but it might mean plenty to his wife. If Vorhees was having an affair with Cory Beckett, it was a possible explanation for the alleged attempt to frame her.

But I was getting ahead of myself. I did not have enough information yet — and most of what I did have was secondhand and hearsay — to form any definite opinions. If I handled things right, I'd know more after some verbal sparring with Cory Beckett.

The Beckett apartment was number 8, top floor front. I rode the elevator up, pushed a pearl bell button. There was a one-way peephole in the door, but Cory Beckett didn't bother to look through it. The door opened almost immediately, wide enough so I could see she was wearing a shimmery lavender silk negligee at one o'clock in the afternoon, and she said, "Did you forget —" before she saw me standing there.

You had to give her credit: her caught-off-guard reaction lasted no more than a couple of seconds. The rounded O of her mouth reshaped into a tentative smile, her body relaxed, and she was back in full control. Or so she thought.

"Oh," she said, "hello. How did you — ?"

"Get in without using the intercom? Andrew Vorhees."

Didn't faze her in the slightest. "I'm sorry?"

"He was leaving the building just as I arrived."

"What would Andrew Vorhees be doing here?"

"Just what I was wondering. Pretty unlikely he'd be visiting somebody else in this building."

She said, not quite challengingly, "And if it was me he came to see? It's really none of your business, is it?" Pause. Then, in a different, eager tone, "Why are *you* here? Do you have news about Kenny?"

She was good, all right. Stonewall, skirt the issue, then a quick shift of subject. I let her get away with it for the time being.

"News, yes," I said.

"You've found him? Where is he?"

"Why don't we talk inside, Ms. Beckett? If you don't mind."

"Yes, of course. Come in."

It was like walking into an abstract art

exhibit. Each wall painted a different primary color, gaudy paintings and wall hangings, multihued chairs and couches, half a dozen gold-flecked mirrors in different shapes and sizes that magnified the riotous color scheme. The place made me uncomfortable, but it also gave me an insight into Cory Beckett. The cool, low-key exterior was pure façade; inside she was like the living space she'd created, with a mind full of flash and intensity and controlled chaos. Her emotional, weak-willed brother must hate this apartment, I thought. So why did he live here with her? Why did she want him to?

After closing the door she made a vague apologetic gesture with one hand, the other holding the top of her negligee closed at her throat. "I'm sorry I'm not dressed. I haven't been feeling well. . . ." Quick change of subject again. "Kenny. You *have* found him, haven't you?"

"One of our operatives has, yes."

"Is he all right?"

"More or less."

"Where is he?"

"Before I tell you, I have some questions."

"Questions? I don't understand."

"About the lies you told in Abe Melikian's office."

"I don't . . . Lies?" Injured innocence now. "I don't have any idea what you mean."

"I think you do. Your brother's alleged amphetamine use, for one. He's not into drugs at all."

"Of course he is — when he's stressed, as I told you. Why would you think otherwise?"

"His word. And no illegal substance of any kind where he's living."

"His word? You spoke to him?"

"Our operative, Jake Runyon, did. Judgment call on his part."

"Then . . . Mr. Runyon's bringing him home?"

"No. Your brother refuses to leave with him. Seems he's not too keen on seeing you again."

"Oh, God, I was afraid of this. That's why I asked that Kenny not be spoken to by anyone but me."

"His version of the theft business is nothing like yours," I said. "He claims Margaret Vorhees' necklace was supposed to be planted in your car, not his van."

"What? Why would I be the intended victim?"

"Because the woman has cause to hate you, he said."

"That's ridiculous. I don't know her except by reputation."

"But you do know her husband."

"Not very well. Hardly at all, in fact."

"Your brother says you were with Vorhees on his yacht that day."

"Did he? Well, I wasn't." She sighed in a put-upon, long-suffering way. "What else did Kenny say?"

"That you talked a man named Chaleen into stashing the necklace in his van."

Her stare had shock in it, just the right amount to be believable. "Why on earth would I do a thing like that?"

"Important to both your futures that he take the blame, your brother claims. Keep from rocking the boat."

"That doesn't many any sense. How could your man Runyon believe such a wild story? Poor Kenny's not stable . . . couldn't he see that? Can't you?"

I didn't say anything.

"He imagines things," she said, "makes up stories that aren't true. What did he say about me? That I don't really care about him, that I force him to do things against his will? That I'm a bad person? Well, that's not so. He's my brother and I love him, I only want what's best for him —"

"Who is Chaleen, Ms. Beckett?"

No response other than two or three eye bats.

"Never heard the name before?"

"I may have, it's vaguely familiar, but . . ." She gnawed at her lower lip for a little time, then in a hesitant, tentative way she walked over to where I stood. Close enough so I could smell the musky perfume she was wearing. Close enough for those luminous eyes of hers to probe intently into mine. "I'm sorry you think badly of me," she said then, "but please, just tell me where Kenny is so I can bring him home."

Nice little performance, not too obvious — she still held the negligee closed at her throat — but I was not fooled by it or affected by her scent or the nearness of her. Vamp stuff doesn't work on me; I've been around too long, seen too much, and I happen to believe in the sanctity of marriage.

I said, "He's at a place called Belardi's on the Petaluma River, about forty miles north of here. Third of three fishing shacks along the shoreline north of the pier. Runyon's there keeping an eye on him."

"Thank you." She held eye contact for a few seconds more; then, when I still showed no signs of responding to the sexual pheromones she was putting out, she produced another of her sad little smiles and slowly backed off. "Now if you'll please leave so I can get dressed. . . ."

I left. It had been an unsatisfactory interview, but Cory Beckett was not easily rattled — practiced liars and deceivers usually aren't — and I'd prodded her as far as I dared.

6

JAKE RUNYON

It was almost three o'clock before Kenneth Beckett's sister showed up at Belardi's.

Nothing happened in the interim. Runyon had gone back inside the shack after the phone conversation with Bill to conduct a careful search for drugs and also for weapons. For all he knew Beckett was suicidal and the last thing he wanted was a dead man on his watch and conscience. He found nothing, not even a sharp knife. Beckett stayed buried under the blanket on the cot, sleeping or just hiding. He hadn't made a sound the entire time.

Outside again, Runyon unlocked the van and poked around among the clutter of tools, paint cans, and other items. Nothing there, either, in the way of weapons or illegal substances.

He did the rest of his waiting in the car. He was used to downtime and he dealt with it as he always did, by putting himself into the equivalent of a computer's sleep mode — a trick he'd learned to help him get through the long months of Colleen's agonizingly slow death. Aware, ready for immediate action if necessary, but otherwise as shut down mentally as he was physically.

Boats passed up and down the river, a few of them stopping at Belardi's dock; cars came and went along Lakeville Highway. Nobody approached the shack until the newish, yellow-and-black Camaro came jouncing along the riverfront track and slid to a stop nearby.

Two occupants, the woman driving and a male passenger. Runyon got out when they did, so that the three of them came together in front of the shack. Cory Beckett was just as Bill had described her, sleek and slender in a white turtleneck sweater and designer jeans, her midnight-black hair tossing in the wind off the marshland. The animal magnetism she possessed was palpable enough, but Runyon would not have responded to it even if he hadn't had the conversation with Kenneth Beckett. The type of woman who attracted him was subtly sexy, like Colleen had been, or lonely, needy, and pain-wracked, like Bryn when he'd first met her. The too-cool, smolderingly seductive type left him cold.

She gave Runyon a long, slow, appraising look, like a prospective buyer sizing up a stud bull. Whether or not she liked what she saw, he couldn't tell. And didn't much care.

She said, "Mr. Runyon? I'm Kenneth's sister, Cory," then gestured in the direction of her companion. "This is a friend I brought along to drive Kenny's van back to the city."

No introduction, just "a friend"; she didn't even look at the man as she spoke. He dipped his chin once, sharply, but said nothing, made no attempt to shake hands. He was in his mid-thirties, sandy-haired, well set up and pretty-boy handsome except for a muscle quirk at one of corner of his mouth that gave the impression of a perpetual sneer in the making.

Runyon said, "Your brother's inside, Ms. Beckett."

"Is he rational? I mean, I understand you talked to him and he told you some wild stories he made up."

Is he rational, not *is he all right.* She seemed less worried about the kid's welfare than about what he might have revealed.

"Calm enough. Withdrawn."

"But not high . . . drugged?"

"No. No sign of drugs on the premises."

"Well, that's a relief. Kenny's much easier to handle when he's sober and tractable." Tractable. Another less-than-concerned word.

Runyon was not about to argue the alleged drug-use issue with her. He shrugged and said nothing.

"I'll get him," she said. "You don't need to wait any longer."

"I'll just make sure he goes along peaceably."

"She told you you don't need to wait," the sandy-haired man said. "If Cory can't handle him, I can."

"I'll wait anyway."

Sandy-hair seemed to want to make an issue of it. The Beckett woman said, "It's all right, Frank," smiled at him the way you might smile at an overly aggressive pet, laid her smoky eyes on Runyon for three or four seconds, and then moved on past him to the door.

He stood watching the shack. Sandy-hair, Frank, paced back and forth on the weedy ground, his hands thrust into the pockets of a light jacket. The electrical wire strung in from the highway, empty now of birds, thrummed in the wind; that was the only sound until Kenneth Beckett let out a cry from inside and then began shouting.

"No, no, I won't, why can't you leave me alone!"

Runyon started toward the shack, but Frank cut over in front of him and grabbed his arm. "Stay out of it," he said. "She can handle him."

"Let go of my arm."

"Yeah? Suppose I don't?"

Runyon jerked loose, started around the man. Combatively Frank moved to block him. They did a little two-step shuffling dance that ended with Frank trying to shove him backward, saying, "Don't mess with me, man, I'll knock you on your ass —"

He half choked on the last word because by then Runyon, in two fast moves, had his arm locked down against his side with forearm and wrist grips. That brought them up tight against each other, their faces a couple of inches apart. Frank worked to struggle free, making growling noises in his throat, but Runyon held him immobile for half a dozen beats before he let go. When he stepped back, it was just far enough to set himself in case Frank had any more aggressive notions.

He didn't. Just glared and rubbed his arm without quite making eye contact again. Runyon had dealt with his type any number of times while on the Seattle PD and since.

A testosterone-heavy hothead, semi-tough until he came up against somebody tougher, more assertive. When that happened, his temper cooled fast and more often than not he'd back down.

Runyon put a little more distance between them before he turned toward the shack. The yelling had stopped; it was quiet in there now. But he went to the door anyway, shoved it open.

The two of them, brother and sister, were standing next to the table, close enough for her to have been putting low-voiced words into his ear. Both looked at Runyon in the open doorway. Kenneth Beckett's face was moist with sweat, but she'd managed to calm him down except for little twitches in his hands, as if they were being manipulated by invisible strings. He looked docile enough in a resigned, trapped way.

"It's all right, Mr. Runyon," the Beckett woman said. "He'll come with me now. Won't you, Kenny?"

He shook his head, twice, but the word that came out of his mouth was, "Yes."

"But you'd better change your clothes first. So you don't get mud all over my car."

"Yeah, okay."

"How did he get so muddy?" she asked Runyon.

"Didn't he tell you?"

"No. He wouldn't say."

"He slipped and fell on the riverbank."

"The riverbank? What happened?"

"Minor panic attack when I got here. He ran out, I ran after him."

Slight frown. "You didn't hit him or anything?"

"I don't operate that way, Ms. Beckett."

"He never touched me," the kid said. "It was my fault. My fault. It's always my fault."

She slipped her arm around his shoulders. "That's enough, now. Go ahead and change your clothes, and I'll pack the rest of your things." Then, to Runyon, "We'll be ready in a few minutes. It's quite all right for you to leave now."

No, it wasn't. He backed out and shut the door to give them privacy. Frank was moving around behind him, walking off his anger and humiliation in tight pacing turns. Runyon went to the Ford, backed it up far enough to allow the van clearance, then switched off the engine and got out to stand next to the driver's door. He didn't move, watching the sandy-haired hothead continue to pace, until the Becketts came out five minutes later.

Kenneth Beckett balked when he saw Frank. "Why'd you have to bring *him*?" he said to his sister.

"I explained that to you inside, Kenny. Somebody has to drive your van back to the city."

"Not him, not Chaleen."

She seemed not to like the fact that he'd used Frank's last name. But all she said was, "Would you rather ride with him than me?"

"No!"

"Then please don't make any more fuss."

Runyon moved over to where the two of them stood. Cory Beckett said, "Really, Mr. Runyon. Why are you still here?"

"Because my job's not finished until you're on your way. And because I have the keys to the van."

He handed them to her. Frank Chaleen came stomping over, the incipient sneer fully formed now, and took the key ring out of her hand. He said to Runyon, "I hope we cross paths again sometime, buddy. Things'll be different then."

"I doubt that."

Chaleen stalked away to the van. Kenneth Beckett said to the middle buttons of Runyon's shirt, "I didn't mean what I said before. About Cory, about the necklace . . . I made it all up. I was kind of disoriented, I didn't know what I was saying."

Runyon said nothing. The kid's words had

a dull, recited cadence, like lines delivered by an amateur actor. Coached, he was thinking, as Cory Beckett led her brother to the Camaro. Part of what she'd been whispering into her brother's ear inside the shack. That, along with Frank Chaleen's presence and attitude, made him even more convinced that what Beckett had told him earlier was the truth.

7

"She's a real piece of work, all right," Tamara said when I finished giving her a short rundown of my interview with Cory Beckett. The woman's apparent involvement with Andrew Vorhees didn't surprise her any more than it had me. "Whatever she's up to, you can bet it's more than just being Vorhees' mistress."

"If she is his mistress."

"Oh, yeah. Her name's on the lease for that Snob Hill apartment, but the monthly rent's fifty-five hundred. She came out of her marriages pretty well fixed, but not well enough to be living it up without some extra juice. Up until six months ago she and Kenny shared a small apartment in Cow Hollow that rented for about two K."

"So you don't think she could have afforded Abe Melikian's five-thousand bond commission and whatever collateral she had to put up for the rest."

"The five K, maybe, but what do you bet Vorhees supplied the collateral. There's blog rumors he's been keeping a woman on the side. Dude's not exactly what you'd call discreet."

"His wife must be a glutton for punishment," I said. "Otherwise, why not divorce instead of separation."

"Still loves the dude. Either that, or she doesn't like to lose what belongs to her."

"And Vorhees doesn't divorce her because?"

"He can't afford to," Tamara said. "Take him right off the gravy train. He's got some money of his own, plus whatever payoffs he can get his hands on, but what lets him own a yacht and live in St. Francis Wood is her money. Inherited. Big bucks."

"Uh-huh. How do you know he collects payoffs?"

"He's a politician, isn't he?"

"You're too young to be so cynical."

"Like I don't have cause? And like you're Mr. Optimist?"

"Okay. Touché."

"Anyhow," she said, "he stays for the money, and screws around because he knows he can get away with it up to a point. Only he crossed some line with Cory Beckett that the wife wouldn't put up with.

Affair getting too public or too involved. Woman like Margaret Vorhees gets jealous enough, she's liable to do anything."

"Such as framing a rival."

"Or having an affair of her own."

"Is that another blog rumor?"

"Yep."

"Sauce for the goose," I said.

"Huh?"

Sometimes I forget young people can be unfamiliar with the old sayings codgers like me grew up on. "Never mind. What else does the blog rumor mill say?"

"This is where it gets juicy. Evidently the dude Mrs. Vorhees had her affair with is Frank Chaleen."

"Well, well. What did you find out about him?"

"He's a peanut vendor."

"A . . . what?"

"Owns a company that makes packing material — you know, plastic peanuts. Chaleen Manufacturing, founded by his late father. Lives high, big bachelor pad in Cow Hollow. Had political ambitions for a while. Hooked up with Andrew Vorhees at some political rally and worked on his campaign for supervisor. But . . . they had a big falling-out about five months ago. Loud face-off one night at the Red Fox, so it made the blogs."

The Red Fox was an expensive downtown restaurant that catered to local politicos. "Because Vorhees found out Chaleen was sleeping with his wife?" I asked.

"Yep. The old double standard. Okay for him to screw around as much as he wants, but not okay for her to be doing it with one of his pals. Apparently he's the one who pushed for the separation, one of those on-again-off-again deals. Mostly he lives on the yacht and she rattles around in the St. Francis Wood house."

I chewed on all of this for a time. Andrew Vorhees, Margaret Vorhees, Cory Beckett, and Frank Chaleen, all tied together in a not-so-neat little package. "Is Chaleen still seeing Mrs. Vorhees?"

"If he is, it's on the sly," Tamara said. "You thinking that's how she got him to help her frame Cory?"

"Could be. Might also explain why she hasn't tried something like it again."

"Only the frame didn't work on account of Cory's ten years younger and has a lot more to offer in the bed department."

"Uh-huh. In which case Chaleen either initiated contact with Cory for that reason, or they were already seeing each other. Maybe met through Vorhees when he and

Chaleen were still tight."

"Must've pissed Cory off big time when she found out she was the target," Tamara said. "Kind of woman *she* is, she's not about to let her meal ticket go without a fight."

"So she jeopardizes her relationship with Vorhees by sleeping and conniving with Chaleen. Why? What kind of fight do you put up by letting your brother get framed instead of you? For that matter, why didn't she just let Vorhees handle the necklace business with his wife and get Kenneth off the hook that way?"

"Maybe that's what not wanting to rock the boat means."

"Still doesn't explain all the scheming."

"Well, Kenny must know or suspect what she's up to. That's why she was so eager to have us find him — get him back home where she can keep an eye on him."

"Can't be the only reason," I said. "She has to have some feelings for him. Took care of him in southern California, lets him live with her here."

"Took care of him when he was a kid, too, after their mama died."

"Which makes her motives all the more inexplicable. She must want him to beat the theft charge, or she wouldn't have hired a high-powered lawyer like Wasserman to defend him."

"Kind of a mind fuck, all right," Tamara said.

I gave her a look, and she grinned and waggled an eyebrow. Old-fashioned workplace decorum defeated once more by the modern penchant for casual obscenity.

"What else did you find out about the Becketts?" I asked.

"Nothing else on Kenny. A few more eyebrow-raisers about her."

"Such as?"

"For one, she got busted one night in L.A. when she was nineteen for lewd and lascivious behavior, soliciting, and contributing to the delinquency of a minor. Got caught with a kid from a rich family she did some nanny work for, fifteen years old, doing the nasty in a public park."

"Where does the soliciting charge come in?"

"Seems she told the kid she'd let him screw her for two hundred bucks. She had the cash in her purse."

"Nice," I said sourly. "Disposition of the case?"

"Wasn't any. All charges dropped before she could be arraigned."

"How come?"

"The kid changed his story about who of-fered the two hundred, said it was him, not her. His old man refused to press the other two charges. So she got off with a wrist-slap fine."

"Why would the father step in that way?"

"Why do you think?" Tamara flashed another impish grin. "Not that there was any hard evidence to prove he was screwing her, too."

I let that pass. "She have any other trouble with the law?"

"One brush, about a year later. Got mixed up with an excon named Hutchinson. Ugly biker dude with weird-ass tats all over him — there's a photo on the Net. Had a list of burglary and armed robbery priors a foot long. Suspected of a couple of murders, too, but the law couldn't prove anything."

"Hutchinson. Beckett mentioned that name to Jake."

"Right. Wonder why. For sure he doesn't have anything to do with what's going on now."

"No? How do you know?"

"Dude's dead. Been dead six years. Shot and killed by the Riverside cops during commission of an armed robbery. Some suspicion Cory was mixed up in a couple of his other crimes right before that, but they couldn't prove it. So she walked."

Evidently Cory Beckett was not in the least discriminating when it came to men. Young, old, handsome, ugly, felons, yachtsmen, and Christ knew what other kind. The only constant seemed to be money — how much an individual had, how much she could get her hands on.

"What's her family background?" I asked.

"Grew up poor in a little town near Riverside," Tamara said. "Father split around the time Kenny was born, mother worked as a housecleaner and died of an aneurysm when Cory was sixteen and Kenny twelve. Kids lived with an aunt for two years, during which time Cory got herself thrown out of high school. No public record of the reason, but you can pretty much figure it had something to do with sex. Right around then she moved out on her own and took her brother with her."

"Supported them how?"

"Nanny jobs with rich folks. Humping for money, too, probably. Made enough to move to Santa Monica. That was when Kenny started working the boating scene. A year after that, she climbed on the big-time marriage-go-round."

"Pretty sorry résumé."

"Say that again. So what do we do about her?"

"Not much we can do, unless Abe Melikian wants us to pursue the matter on his behalf."

"Not him. All he cares about is not losing his bond money."

I wasn't so sure about that, given the way he'd fawned over Cory Beckett in his office; but then again, he'd always been a businessman first and foremost. "In that case, we'll have to drop it. You know we can't continue an investigation without a client."

"Yeah. Damn, though. I'd sure like to know what that woman's up to."

"So would I," I said. "After the fact, with nobody hurt, and from a safe distance."

Abe Melikian was another Saturday workaholic, in his office and busy with a client when I rang up. I told the staff member I spoke to to let him know I had news for him and would deliver it in person within the hour.

Runyon checked in as I was about to leave the agency, with the news that Cory Beckett had brought Frank Chaleen along with her to Belardi's. The woman was brazen as hell. Lied in her teeth to me about not knowing Chaleen, then as soon as I was gone, called

Chaleen in to help her fetch her brother home.

As Tamara had predicted, Melikian didn't want us to do any more investigating. He was upset that we'd probed into her background as much as we had. He already knew that Kenneth Beckett had been found and Cory was bringing him back well ahead of his trial date because she'd called to tell him so, and why the hell hadn't I notified him right away myself instead of going to her apartment and harassing her?

I tried to explain about her background, her ties to Vorhees and Chaleen, the lies and manipulations we'd uncovered, but I might as well have been talking to a statue. He refused to consider that she might be anything other than the selfless sister she pretended to be; kept defending her and her intentions. Kenneth Beckett was unstable, he said, parroting what she'd told me; the kid's sudden run-out proved that, didn't it? The story he'd told Runyon was "a load of drug-raving bullshit." Cory had her brother's best interests at heart, was doing everything she could to keep him out of prison.

Old Abe was hooked, all right. So deeply hooked that I couldn't help wondering if she was sleeping with him, too. He was always paying lip service to family and family values — he'd been married thirty years, had two grown daughters and a son in high school — and I had taken him for a straight arrow. But when a sexy piece half a man's age makes herself available to him, the temptation for some can be too strong to resist. Not for me, and never with a woman like Cory Beckett — that's what I told myself. I hadn't succumbed in her apartment, but how could I be absolutely sure I wouldn't under different circumstances?

I said, "Okay, Abe. Have it your way. We'll back off."

"Damn well better. Beckett's back, I'm not gonna lose my bond — case closed. You want any more business from me, stay the hell away from Cory and her brother."

So that's the end of it, I thought. Kenneth Beckett gets convicted or acquitted at his trial, his sister goes right on lying, manipulating, using men to her own ends, and we forget the whole sorry business and move on. Case closed.

Only it wasn't.

No, not by a long shot.

8

KENNETH BECKETT

He didn't know what to do.

Scared all the time now. Scared of the trial, scared of going to prison, but mostly scared of Cory.

She didn't trust him anymore. Made him give her his car keys, wouldn't let him go out alone after dark, locked him in his room at night when she went off with Mr. Vorhees or that bastard Chaleen. She said it was just until after the trial, for his own safety, even though he'd promised he wouldn't skip out again like he had when she flew to Las Vegas with Mr. Vorhees and left him all alone. Well, maybe it was for his own good, but did she have to treat him like he was a snot-nosed kid? Or worse, a half-wit the way Chaleen did?

She wouldn't confide in him anymore, either. Or give him a hint of what her plans were. She had secrets again. Her and Chaleen. Ugly secrets, crazy secrets. He was sure of that much.

She was out with Chaleen now, in the middle of the afternoon. Hadn't said that was where she was going, just said she'd be out for a while, but he'd heard her on the phone through her bedroom door before she left and it was plain enough who she was talking to.

He didn't understand it. What did she want Chaleen for? She had a good thing going with Mr. Vorhees, a decent guy to work for, a guy who treated her right — bought her things, gave her money to help pay the rent on the apartment. Mr. Vorhees treated him decent, too, never talked down to him. Tried to get his wife to drop the theft charge, but Cory said the woman was too full of hate to listen to reason. Sure, Mr. Vorhees was still married, but legally separated, and Cory'd had affairs with married men before — "I don't subscribe to society's moral standards," that was always her excuse. Besides, she said, it was different with Mr. Vorhees because he loved her and she loved him and they were going to get married after his wife was out of the picture. So why was she risking everything by sneaking off and letting Chaleen do it to her, too?

She'd turned into a different person since they moved to San Francisco. Most of the time they'd lived in Marina del Rey and Newport Beach, she'd been loving and kind and caring, but now she was back to being the wild thing she'd been when that other bastard, Hutchinson, got his hooks into her. Or maybe she'd been that way all along, just didn't let him see it.

He didn't like that Cory at all. Lying to him. Telling people he used drugs when he never had. Making him do crazy, hurtful things like being arrested for stealing Mrs. Vorhees' necklace and then not explaining why, just saying over and over, "Don't worry, Kenny, don't I always do what's best for us?"

No, she *didn't* always do what was best. She'd done a lot of crazy stuff he knew about and probably some he didn't. Like messing with that damn rich teenager in L.A. for money. And all the sick shit with Hutchinson. And treating poor Mr. Lassiter so bad he'd ended up killing himself. That wasn't her fault, she said, she had no idea he was suicidal, but it *was* her fault. Sneaking around with other guys, taking money she wasn't supposed to have, fighting with the man all the time. Maybe she'd even planned it. There was something kind of funny about the night Mr. Lassiter died, too — Cory making him say he was there with her in the house when it happened, when she and Mr. Lassiter had been alone together. The lie was to keep people from getting the wrong idea, she'd said, and he believed her, but still it bothered him whenever he thought about it.

All these things preying on his mind scared him, made him nervous as hell. He couldn't sit still, just kept prowling the apartment. It wasn't so bad when Cory went away at night and locked him in, not that she had to do that — he knew he had to stay in the city now, he was resigned to it, so he just watched TV or read one of his nautical books until she came home or he went to sleep.

But it was different when he was by himself like this during the day, free but not free. He could go out if he wanted to, but the trouble was, he had nowhere to go. Well, down to the yacht club to look at the boats, Cory was okay with that, but he had to tell her ahead of time in order to get the bus fare. She wouldn't let him have any money otherwise, and he didn't have any now. The only other thing he could do was walk around the neighborhood, up and down the steep hills, and all that did was make him more nervous, more restless.

God, he wished he had somebody to talk to besides Cory. A friend he could unload his troubles to, who'd understand what he was going through and maybe give him an idea of what to do. He might've been able to talk to Mr. Vorhees, but Cory wouldn't let him on account of that damn necklace. Even somebody like the guy who'd found him at Belardi's might be okay if he wasn't a detective — he'd told Mr. Runyon more that day than he'd ever thought he could tell anybody, it had just come spilling out of him. He'd had a couple of casual buddies in Newport Beach, but they were just guys who worked in the marina like he did, guys he could have a beer and talk boats with. Up here he didn't even have anyone like that. Hadn't made one single friend in San Francisco. Except for Cory he was alone, all alone.

Cory, Cory, Cory!

Her bedroom door was unlocked. He went in even though he wasn't supposed to without permission. The sexy perfume she'd put on for Chaleen was sweet in the air, sickening sweet. It made him think of her and that bastard together in bed, Chaleen sweating and grunting on top of her, and he felt like gagging. He shoved the ugly images

90

out of his mind.

What were they planning? He thought it might have something to do with Mrs. Vorhees, a way to stop her from testifying against him and sending him to prison, and he hoped that was it, but at the same time he was afraid of what it might be.

He moved around Cory's room, the master bedroom. She'd always made a big deal out of him respecting her privacy, but he couldn't stop himself from invading it now. He didn't really believe there was anything here that'd give him an idea of what she and Chaleen were up to, but how did you know for sure unless you looked?

He opened the drawer in the nightstand next to the king-size bed, and the first thing he saw was a package of condoms she kept in there. Right away he slammed it shut again and went over to her vanity table. Those drawers were full of cosmetics, and the ones in the red Chinese dresser were stuffed with silky underwear in the bright colors she liked. The walk-in closet was packed, too: racks of expensive shoes, coats, suits, dresses — five times as many nice clothes as he owned. Different size cartons and boxes jammed the shelf above. What was in them?

He took one down, opened it. Fancy

round cloth hat with a tiny brim. Nobody wore hats anymore, did they? He'd never seen Cory in this one or any other. He put it back, took down another carton. New cowhide boots that probably wouldn't fit on the rack. He exchanged that carton for a smaller one with an Emporio Armani label on it. See-through nightgown. He put that away quickly, reached for a small, square box in one corner. Something hard wrapped in a cloth. . . .

His breath sucked in when he saw what it was. New, too, brand new, and so small and cold he almost let go of it, the way you would a live thing that might suddenly bite. He stared at it, the fear and confusion in him growing.

"Kenny!"

He jumped at the sound of his name, swung around. She was standing in the bedroom doorway, her face clouded with fury. He'd been so focused on what he'd found he hadn't heard her come into the apartment — she always walked quick and silent like a cat.

"Oh, God, Cory —"

Her expression darkened even more when she saw what he was holding. She came fast to where he was, snapped, "Give me that," and snatched it out of his hand, then slapped him across the face, hard. "What do you think you're doing in my bedroom, pawing through my possessions? You know how much I hate that."

He fingered his stinging cheek. "I'm sorry, I just . . . I . . ."

"Now I'll have to lock my bedroom door, too, when I go out so you won't sneak around in here anymore."

"Cory, why do you have a —"

"Never mind. It's none of your concern. Forget about it, forget you ever saw it. You understand me, Kenny?"

". . . Yes."

"All right. Now get out of here. Go to your room and stay there."

In his room, he lay on the bed staring up at the ceiling. His hands felt damp, clammy. His cheek still burned where she'd slapped him.

Forget about it, she'd said. But how could he?

A gun. Jesus, what was she doing with a gun?

9

JAKE RUNYON

It was a couple of minutes past seven on Wednesday evening when Runyon pulled up in front of Bryn's brown-shingle house on Moraga in the outer Sunset. Lights glowed behind the front windows, which meant she and Bobby were home now. She never wasted electricity when the two of them were out. He scooped the shopping bag from the passenger seat, went up and rang the bell.

Bryn opened the door, evidently without checking through its peephole. She was smiling, but the smile dimmed when she saw Runyon. Expecting someone else, he thought, and her first words confirmed it.

"Jake. What are you doing here?"

"Dropping off Bobby's birthday present."

"Oh, you remembered. Well, he'll be pleased." Not her so much, though, he thought; the smile was almost gone now.

"But you should have called first. You always have before."

"I did call," Runyon said, "around five-thirty. No answer. I thought you might have taken the boy out for an early dinner to celebrate."

"No, we were at Safeway. Why didn't you leave a message on my cell?"

"Didn't think of it. Didn't think you'd mind if I just dropped in."

"I don't, only . . ." She shook her head. "Never mind. Come in."

Inside, in the hallway light, he saw that she wasn't as casually dressed as she usually was when she intended to stay in. Starched white blouse, green patterned skirt, a cameo locket at her throat, and a gold bracelet on one wrist. Ash-blond hair neatly combed and decorated with a ribbon that matched her skirt. Lipstick, too, and a little eye makeup. The scarf covering the stroke-frozen left side of her face was the paisley one Bobby had picked out, in Runyon's company, for her last birthday.

He said, "If you're going out again, I won't keep you."

"We're having dinner here. I'd invite you to stay, but . . . well, it's not a good time."

"Company coming?"

"As a matter of fact, yes." Four-beat.

"Robert."

Runyon was silent.

"He called and asked if he could come," Bryn said with a defensive note in her voice. "He has presents, too, and after all, he is the boy's father."

And the man who had divorced Bryn when she suffered her crippling and disfiguring stroke, the man who had used his attorney's influence to take Bobby away from her and into the clutches of the unstable woman who'd been his mistress, the man she claimed to hate and had fought bitterly, with Runyon's help, to regain custody.

He said only, "Sure."

"Robert's been nice to the boy, much kinder than when Bobby was living with him." The defensiveness was more pronounced now. "It's hard to believe, but he's changed since Francine was murdered. Oh, he's still arrogant, still the typical lawyer, but the nastiness and cruelty . . . they seem to be gone."

"Showing signs of humanity."

"Yes, exactly. And he truly loves Bobby, cares about his future."

"Never much doubt of that."

"So when we . . . So I didn't see any reason not to invite him to stay for dinner."

96

Runyon said, "No need to justify it to me."

"I wasn't justifying, I was simply stating a fact."

"All right."

"I'm not getting involved with him again, if that's what you're thinking."

It wasn't. "None of my business in any case."

"No. I just wanted you to know."

"All right."

But she couldn't seem to let it go. "Neither Robert nor I wants to get back together," she said. Threads of defiance, now, in her voice. "I wouldn't take him back if he got down on his knees and begged me. He hurt me too much, there's been too much anger and bitterness between us. You know all that. We've talked about it often enough."

"Yes."

"He'll be here pretty soon," she said.

"Then I'd better leave." Runyon extended the shopping bag. "You can give this to Bobby and wish him a happy birthday from me."

Bryn hesitated. "No, he should have it from you. He'll want to thank you personally. He's in his room — I'll fetch him."

She hurried away to the rear of the house. Standing still while he waited made Runyon fidget; he moved over to the living room doorway. Soft music was playing in there, one of the quieter classical pieces Bryn favored. A tray of canapés had been set out on the coffee table, and there were three or four gaily wrapped presents — her birthday tribute to Bobby — neatly arranged on one end of the couch. He stepped back into the hallway, slow-paced back and forth until Bryn returned with her son.

Bobby was ten today. He'd grown another half inch or so since Runyon had first met him, still a gangly kid who would probably stand well over six feet when he reached his full growth, his hair longer now and combed in a more conventional fashion than the spikily gelled style he'd favored back then. He hadn't lost any of his shyness, at least not around Runyon. He was smiling and seemed glad to see him, but there was a reserve in both his greeting and his off-center gaze. The bond that had developed between them during Runyon's investigation of the brutal murder of Francine Whalen, Robert Darby's mistress cum fiancée, and that had lasted for a while after Bryn won the second court battle for the boy's custody, hadn't been strong enough to last. Devolved into a polite and increasingly distant relationship as they spent less and less time in each other's company.

Bryn steered them away from the living room and into the dining room — table set for three, crystal glassware and good china — and the aromas of something cooking in the oven wafting in from the kitchen. Bobby opened his gift at the cleared end of the table. Two Nintendo video games, Star Fox Command and Metroid Prime Hunters, that the salesman in the computer store in Stonestown had recommended to Runyon. The boy seemed pleased with them, and his thanks was genuine enough, but it lacked any real excitement and only a tepid warmth. Probably saving his enthusiasm for whatever his mother had given him, whatever his father brought.

A brief hug, and Bobby took the video games away to his room. Bryn cast a look at her wristwatch for the third or fourth time. Runyon said, "Don't worry, I'll be going now."

"I wasn't worried," she said, trying not to look relieved, "it's just that it would be awkward. You don't like Robert and he doesn't like you. . . ."

"No need to explain."

She went with him to the front door. "Jake," she said as he started out, looking past him to the empty street. "Next time, call first before you come over. Okay?"

"I will."

But he wouldn't, because there wouldn't be a next time. He knew it and so did Bryn.

Their relationship, even the friendship part that had included Bobby, had come to an abrupt and irredeemable end.

Home for Runyon since his move to San Francisco was a drafty, sparsely furnished, one-bedroom apartment on Ortega Street, off Nineteenth Avenue. His first actions when he let himself in were habitual, done each night without thinking: turn the heat up, switch the TV on for noise, put a kettle on to boil for tea, check the landline answering machine and his laptop for messages. No calls, no e-mail that needed an immediate reply.

In the refrigerator he found a package of Swiss cheese slices and another of pressed ham that hadn't gone green yet, buttered two pieces of stale but still edible bread, and made himself a sandwich he didn't want. His appetite was light at the best of times and the scene with Bryn had killed what little hunger he'd had tonight, but you had to eat. The human engine, like the mechanical one in the Ford, wouldn't run long or far without regular injections of fuel.

When the tea was ready, he took cup and

sandwich into the living room and ate in front of the TV. Old movies were all that he watched because he wasn't into sports and everything else had endless commercials, laugh tracks, halfwits making fools of themselves in so-called reality shows, bogus cops solving sensationalistic hour-long psychodramas, and macho types firing off automatic weapons, blowing up cars and buildings, and spilling excess amounts of blood and gore. The only vintage film showing at the moment, an old musical with Bing Crosby, didn't hold his attention. The final split with Bryn was still on his mind.

Not that it had had much of an emotional effect on him. The finish had been coming for some time now. Tonight had been nothing more than a kind of pro forma goodbye.

Her ex-husband wasn't a major factor, just the catalyst that had snapped the last connecting thread. Didn't really matter, but Runyon couldn't help wondering if she'd take Darby back on a temporary or permanent basis. Possible, he supposed. That old fine line between love and hate: one that had turned into the other could turn back again if the circumstances were right. How much Darby had changed, how remorseful he was, how willing and able to

101

deal now with her facial paralysis. And the deciding factor: how much Bobby would benefit from a reconciliation. The boy's welfare was first and foremost to Bryn and always would be.

Whatever her feelings for Darby, whatever her plans for the future, they no longer included Jake Runyon. That much was clear. She'd needed him desperately for a while, and in his bitter loneliness he'd needed her almost as much. But the bad time for both of them was over, past history. She'd always be grateful for his help in regaining custody of her son, but gratitude only went so far. There'd never been much else between them except the mutual damage control, nothing deep enough to cement a lasting bond. Now that she and Bobby were a solid package deal again, having Runyon around was probably a painful reminder of a period of suffering that had brought her to the brink of self-destruction. Time to burn her bridges, time to move on.

He'd miss her a little, but nowhere near as much as he missed Colleen. Miss Bobby, too — a nice, sensitive kid, the kind of son he'd like to have had. But the missing would be only temporary. The truth was, Bobby had never been and could never be anything more than a surrogate for Joshua, his own painful reminder of the failed relationship with his son. Bobby was better off without him; he was better off without Bobby. Better off alone, now that he'd made some measure of peace with himself. . . .

When the phone rang — his landline, not his cell — his first thought, because he'd been thinking of her, was that it might be Bryn. He came close to not answering it. They had nothing more to say to each other, and the only other landline calls at this time of night were either wrong numbers or late-lurking telemarketers.

Wrong on all counts. He picked up on the sixth ring, mainly to shut off the clamor, and a man's thin, nervous-sounding voice, unfamiliar at first, said tentatively, "Mr. Runyon?"

"If you're selling something —"

"No. I remembered your name, I looked in the phone book. . . ."

He recognized the voice then. "Ken Beckett?"

"Yeah. I . . . I have to talk to somebody, Mr. Runyon. I don't know anyone else."

"What's on your mind?"

Pause. Then, "Not on the phone, okay? I can't talk about this on the phone."

"Are you home? I can come there —"

"No! Cory's out now, but she might come

back any time."

"Meet me somewhere, then."

"I can't do that, either. She locks me in at night when she goes out."

"Every time?"

"Yes."

Runyon said, "Can you get out during the daytime?"

"I think so. She lets me go down to the yacht club in the morning if she's in a good mood. On the bus."

"Which yacht club?"

"Where I used to work. The St. Francis."

Runyon thought it over. He had a case interview scheduled in the morning, but it could be postponed. From the stressed-out sound of Beckett's voice, whatever he had to say was important.

"All right, Ken. What time in the morning?"

"Ten o'clock, is that okay?"

"Name a place to meet. I'll be there."

"Just you? Nobody else?"

"Just me."

More silence. Then, "I have to be careful. If she finds out, I don't know what she might do. . . ."

"You can trust me. I don't betray confidences."

That satisfied Beckett. "You know the big

green clock in front of the St. Francis, right by the parking lot?"

"I can find it."

"Thanks, Mr. Runyon. I'll see you at ten." Then, as if to himself before he broke the connection, "I can't be alone anymore."

10

JAKE RUNYON

Even on a weekday morning, the Marina Green and the area along the West Harbor yacht basin was packed with joggers, women pushing baby strollers, adults and children on benches and grass taking advantage of the warming sun. Runyon had driven down early because parking at the only part of the Green he'd been to before, near Gashouse Cove and Fort Mason, was at a premium and he'd figured the same might be true at the opposite end. Not so. There were plenty of spaces in the lot on Yacht Road near the St. Francis. So he had twenty minutes to kill until ten o'clock.

The big green clock Beckett had mentioned was easy to spot — a Roman-numeral Rolex atop an old-fashioned standard a dozen feet tall, standing between the parking lot and the tan, Spanish-style yacht club. A rocky seawall ran behind the club on the bay side; stretched out in front was the West Harbor basin where club members' boats were berthed, a thin forest of masts extending out to Marina Boulevard. In that direction you could see the Golden Gate Bridge and the big sunlit dome of the Palace of Fine Arts.

Runyon was too restless to stand waiting there for twenty minutes. He went the other direction, through a break in the seawall and along a bayfront walkway. From there, if you cared, you had a clear look at the wide sweep of the bay where a few sailboats tacked along and a tourist boat was headed out toward Alcatraz. He paid little attention. Scenic views and panoramas didn't interest him anymore; hadn't since Colleen's death. He noted landmarks to orient himself or for future reference. Otherwise, places were just places, colorless, void of any distinction or attraction.

He got rid of fifteen minutes on the bayfront walk. Beckett still hadn't showed when he returned to the clock, so he crossed to the concrete strip that ran along the harbor's upper edge. Wandered a short distance past sailboats, yachts, other large craft in their slips, then back again.

A little after ten, and Beckett still hadn't put in an appearance. Runyon did some more pacing around under the clock.

Five minutes, ten minutes. He was beginning to wonder if the kid had changed his mind when Beckett finally showed, hurrying along the far edge of the boat basin. Not quite running but moving fast, head down, arms pumping like pistons.

Runyon moved to meet him at the top of the parking lot. He didn't look much better than he had at the shack at Belardi's. Pale, nervous, bagged and blood-flecked eyes indicating sleepless nights. The eyes briefly held on Runyon's, flicked away, flicked back, flicked away.

"Sorry I'm late, Mr. Runyon," he said. "She almost didn't let me go out today. I had to promise to be back by noon."

"Why?"

"We're meeting with Mr. Wasserman, the lawyer, this afternoon. And having an early dinner with . . ." Beckett let the rest of what he'd been about to say trail off. "Let's go over by the slips, okay?"

Runyon followed him to the walkway, where Beckett leaned on the iron railing above the slips. At intervals along here, ramps led down to locked gates that barred public access to the moored craft. Beckett gestured at the nearest gate and said in hurt tones, "They won't let me in anymore. Mr.

Voorhees took away my key."

Runyon made a sympathetic noise.

"I really liked working for him, you know? You ever see his yacht?"

"No."

"It's down a ways, this side." Beckett set off again in quick, jerky strides. After a couple of hundred yards he stopped and pointed. "There she is, the *Ocean Queen*. Isn't she a beauty?"

Runyon looked. All he saw was a yacht — big, sleek, expensive. But in Beckett's eyes it was a pot of gold at the end of somebody else's rainbow.

"Man, I wish I had a baby like that," he said with a kind of wistful hunger. "Maritimo 73, eighty-one footer with a twenty-one-foot beam, two Caterpillar C32 engines, thirty knots cruising speed. Sweet. But Mr. Vorhees doesn't take her out as often as he should. If I owned her, I'd be cruising all the time. All the time."

Runyon let him gawk and pine a few more seconds before yanking him back to reality. "What did you want to talk to me about, Ken?"

"What? Oh, God." The kid's thin features seemed to curl and reshape themselves, like a Play-Doh face being manipulated between unseen hands. Misery replaced the wistfulness in his eyes and voice.

"Something to do with your sister?"

"She has a gun," Beckett said.

"A gun. What kind of gun?"

"Little one, with a squarish barrel and pearl handles. She never had one before, she never liked guns."

A .22 or .25 caliber automatic, probably. Purse weapon.

"Where did she get it?"

"I don't know. It's new, I think she bought it."

"Did she show it to you?"

"No, I found it in her closet. Two days ago. She told me to forget about it, but I . . . I can't. Not after what I heard her saying on the phone yesterday."

"Who was she talking to?"

"That bastard Chaleen. She's planning something bad with him."

"Only you don't know exactly what, is that it?"

"Yeah. I mean no. She was in her bedroom, talking low — I couldn't hear everything she said. Plans, she always has plans, but she won't tell me what they are. 'Everything will be all right, Kenny, you'll see. Haven't I always taken care of you?' Yes, but not always the way she promised she would."

"Like letting you go to jail for a crime you didn't commit."

"Like that, yeah."

"What else?"

No response.

"Like getting you to help her meet rich yachtsmen? Her ex-husbands, Andrew Vorhees."

"Jesus. You know about her and Mr. Vorhees?"

Runyon nodded.

"She says she loves him and he loves her," Beckett said. "I guess that's so, I don't know. He's okay, Mr. Vorhees, he always treated me decent, and we need the money he gives Cory. I understand that. But I don't understand why she has to have Chaleen, too. It's like a game with her . . . one and then another and then somebody else. . . ."

"Does Mr. Vorhees know about her and Chaleen?"

"No. He'd be pissed if he did. Real pissed."

Runyon said, "Tell me exactly what your sister said on the phone. Everything you can remember."

" 'Bitch deserves it for what she did.' " That mimicking falsetto again. " 'Be careful, darling, no mistakes. So much at stake for both of us once she's out of the way.' "

"Who did she mean by 'bitch'?"

"Mrs. Vorhees."

"Mentioned her by name?"

"No, but I know that's who she meant."

Not conclusively, he didn't. "Did Cory say when whatever it is is going to happen?"

"Soon. Sometime soon."

"But not exactly when?"

"No." Beckett drew a long, shaky breath. Then, in a half whisper, "Even after what Mrs. Vorhees did, I don't want them to hurt her. I don't want anybody to be hurt."

"Of course you don't. Neither do I."

"That's why I called you, Mr. Runyon. I didn't know what else to do. Cory's done a lot of bad things, but I never thought she was capable of . . . of . . ." The word *murder* was in his mouth, his lips shaping it, but he couldn't bring himself to say it aloud.

"Does she know you overheard her conversation?"

"God, no. She'd've yelled at me if she did. And pretended I didn't hear what I heard. She says she never lies to me but she does, all the time now. She lies to everybody. She's my sister, I love her, but sometimes I think she's a little, you know, a little crazy."

Runyon had nothing to say to that.

Beckett seemed to make an effort to pull himself together. He said, "Mr. Runyon?

Will you stop her and Chaleen from hurting Mrs. Vorhees?"

"If I can, yes." He got out a business card with both his cell and landline numbers on it, pressed it into Beckett's hand. "If you find out anything more, call me right away, day or night."

"Right away. Yes."

"And be careful not to let on to your sister that you've been talking to me."

"Don't worry, I will."

Runyon left him standing there staring at Andrew Vorhees' yacht and the boats in the West Harbor slips, his mouth shaping more words that he couldn't or wouldn't speak aloud.

11

Thursday was a hell of a miserable day.

The kind that makes you think, not nearly for the first time in my case, that free will is a load of crap and your life really isn't your own. That Shakespeare was right and we're all just players on a vast stage, being secretly moved around and fed lines to speak and actions to take by some unseen director. Or part of an ecumenical puppet show: marionettes controlled by an impossible-to-comprehend webwork of invisible strings and threads and wires. Or, worse, not even flesh and blood human beings but androids programmed and manipulated by impulses from some all-powerful mega-computer operated by an entity or entities beyond our ken. The devout among us call it God's Plan — the Almighty working in mysterious ways His wonders to perform. But I'm not convinced it's as simple or benign as that. Or that it's benign at all.

Such days usually follow a pattern: they start out in ordinary fashion and then grow progressively worse. This one was no exception. I woke up in a pretty good mood; so did Kerry, so did Emily. The three of us had a companionable breakfast, even did a little joking around the way close-knit family units often do. I kissed Kerry and off she went to Bates and Carpenter, kissed Emily and off she went to school. Then I had the place to myself — one of my stay-at-home days, with nothing more demanding to do, or so I thought, than to devote some more time to my pulp collection.

I was involved in that project when Jake Runyon called in a report of his meeting and conversation with Kenneth Beckett, a call that began the day's shift from commonplace to dark and hellish. Trying to decide, when the phone rang, if I could afford a hundred bucks for a 1932 issue of *Dime Detective* with an Erle Stanley Gardner novelette, one of only two issues from that year that I didn't own. The price was not too bad on the current collector's market and the dealer making the offer was a man I'd bought from before; the sticking point was the magazine's condition, which he described as "near very good with a piece missing from the spine." He'd provided color scans in his e-mail, but looking at scans isn't the same thing as holding a magazine in your hands for a close inspection.

Jake's report put me in something of a quandary. I didn't blame him for getting together with the Beckett kid — I'd have done the same if I had been on the receiving end of the plea for help — but what he'd been told about a conspiracy between Cory Beckett and Frank Chaleen created an ethical and moral dilemma. Officially, we had no standing in the matter. No client, no evidence to support the suspicions of an emotionally damaged young man, which for all we knew for certain were nothing more than delusional ravings. Nor could we justify notifying the police. If the allegations of a plot to harm Margaret Vorhees turned out to be unfounded, we'd be wide open for a potentially ruinous lawsuit.

That was the ethical and legal side of it. The moral duty side was something else again. In all good conscience, you couldn't afford not to alert a potential victim when you had enough familiarity with the other people concerned to make premeditated homicide a very real possibility.

Runyon agreed. He thought he ought to stay on it, maybe have a talk with Mrs.

Vorhees and alert her to the potential danger. I didn't much like the idea — ticklish business, approaching somebody out of the blue with a story like that and not very much to back it up, because it could so easily backfire — but I couldn't and didn't reject it, either. What I did was to put Runyon's suggestion on hold for the time being. He had other work to do, and the final decision was mine and Tamara's.

I hemmed and hawed with myself for a time. Then, with my mind pretty much made up, I called Tamara. For support, mainly, because I knew what her position would be. As young as she is, and despite a somewhat checkered past, she has a moral outlook similar to mine and Runyon's.

"Damn right we should do something," she said. "Sooner the better. I say take what we know to Mrs. Vorhees and see what she says."

"That was Jake's suggestion."

"You agree?"

"Leaning that way."

"Okay, then. Might even be she'll hire us to protect her." Moral, my partner, but ever practical. "Yeah, I know we're not set up for bodyguard work, but we could make an exception in this case."

"If it comes to that, we'll consider it."

"Think I should be the one to talk to her, woman to woman?"

Tamara has plenty of strong points, but caution and tact are two that she hasn't quite mastered yet. And when you were dealing with a prominent citizen who was also a vindictive alcoholic, you had to be extra careful. I said, "Better let me handle it."

"Jake's the one who talked to Kenny. Maybe he should do it."

I reminded her that Runyon had an appointment in the East Bay and was already on his way. "I'm old enough to be nonthreatening to most people," I said. The patriarchal approach might just get through to her, if I worked it right. Besides, it was my case, or it had started out that way anyhow. "I'll need Margaret Vorhees' phone numbers, land and cell both."

Tamara didn't put up any further argument. She tracked down the numbers for me in short order.

I tried the cell first, but the call went straight to voice mail. I clicked off without leaving a message and rang Margaret Vorhees' home phone. That call was answered by a woman with a Spanish accent who informed me she was the housekeeper. Yes, Mrs. Vorhees was home, but she was busy and couldn't come to the phone. The way she said the word "busy," in a faintly disapproving tone, made me wonder if her employer might be getting an early start on her day's drinking. Did I wish to leave a message? No, I didn't. If I left my name and number, chances were I would not get a callback. And I didn't want to lay out my bona fides except to Mrs. Vorhees herself, in person.

Her home was only a couple of miles from our Diamond Heights condo. I decided I might as well drive over there and see if I could maneuver my way into an audience with the woman.

Like Nob Hill, St. Francis Wood, on the lower western slope of Mount Davidson, is one of the city's best residential neighborhoods: near-palatial old homes on large lots that you couldn't afford to buy unless your net worth was counted in the millions. The Vorhees house stood on a tree-shaded street not far from the home once owned by George Moscone, the San Francisco mayor who'd been assassinated along with Supervisor Harvey Milk back in the seventies. Spanish Mission-style place, all stucco and dark wood and terra-cotta tile, tucked back behind tall hedges and a procession of yucca

119

trees. A line of eucalyptus ran along the west side. The overall effect was of a kind of mini-estate that somewhat diminished the stature of its neighbors.

I followed a winding flagstone path that led from the front gate onto a tiled porch. The front door was of heavy dark wood mortised with strips of metal, a bell button set into the tile alongside. A thumb on the button produced musical chimes loud enough to be heard through the stucco walls.

Pretty soon the door opened on a chain and a plump brown face peered out at me — the Latina maid I'd spoken to on the phone. When I asked for Margaret Vorhees, she offered up the same "busy" message and started to close the door. My foot was in the way by then. I passed one of my cards through the opening and said through a grave professional smile, "Please take this to Mrs. Vorhees and tell her it's urgent I speak with her on a matter involving her stolen necklace."

The maid looked at me as if she didn't quite comprehend the message. Or pretended she didn't. So I repeated it in Spanish. My command of the language is passably good because Spanish is similar to Italian, which had been spoken in my home every day while I was growing up. The use of her native tongue did the trick. She nodded and said, *"Espere por favor aqui,"* in a more respectful tone, and on that obliging note I removed my foot and let her close the door.

The wait was maybe five minutes. A couple of cars drifted by on the street, the wind made rattling noises in the eucalyptus; otherwise the neighborhood seemed wrapped in stillness. Money can buy peace and quiet as well as luxury and privacy. Sometimes.

When the maid returned, the chain rattled and the door opened all the way to let me in. I followed her along a dark, terra-cotta hallway into an equally dark living room, where she asked me again in Spanish to please wait and then left me alone.

Thick patterned drapes were drawn over the windows; the only light came from a floor lamp set between a couple of heavy wood-framed couches set at right angles to each other. Against one wall was a massive, ornately carved sideboard on which an array of liquor bottles and crystal glasses gleamed on silver trays. The rest of the furniture was the same heavy, baroque Spanish style. No television set or other modern touches, just the collection of expensive antiques arranged on a dark-patterned carpet.

The only real color in the room was on the walls — half a dozen paintings, a rough-woven, blanket-like affair like an oversized serape — and what there was of it was in muted hues. The overall effect was one of oppressive gloom. Spend much time in here and you'd start to feel claustrophobic, maybe even a touch suicidal. If this was where Margaret Vorhees did most of her home-front drinking, as the booze on the sideboard indicated, then she must be a pretty depressed individual.

I was looking at one of the paintings, a court scene signed by Diego Velázquez that was probably a copy, or then again maybe not, when a swishing sound turned me around. She came sweeping in from the hallway, like a diva making an entrance — a diva who might have been in mourning, given the fact that she was wearing a loose black pantsuit that matched her coiled black hair. The only color on her was too much bright red lipstick, less than artfully applied, that made her mouth look like a bloody smear.

At a distance she had a slender, regal bearing, and a kind of pale, patrician beauty, but as she advanced toward me I could see the signs of dissipation. She was on the near side of forty, but already the skin on her high cheek-boned face had lost its firmness and you could see the beginnings of puffy folds under her chin. The regal bearing was an illusion, too; her movements were the stiff, careful ones of the practiced drunk intent on simulating sobriety. The too-red mouth had a kind of crooked laxity and it wasn't smiling.

She stopped about three feet from where I stood. Her arms were down at her sides and she kept them there: no offer of a handshake. She looked me up and down for maybe fifteen seconds. Nothing changed in her expression, and it was too dark in there to read her eyes, but I had the impression she didn't much like what she saw. The first words she spoke confirmed it.

"Private detective," she said, the way you'd identify a large bug. Cold voice, careful enunciation without a trace of slur. "Who sent you?"

"No one sent me, Mrs. Vorhees."

"I suppose it was Cory Beckett," she said, as if I hadn't spoken. "That's whom you're working for, isn't it?"

"Not any longer. I was retained by Ms. Beckett and her brother's bail bondsman —"

"To do what? Help keep her brother from going to jail for stealing my necklace?"

"In a way, yes."

"What way?"

"That's privileged information."

"Privileged," she said, making it sound like a dirty word. Then she said, "That poor young fool. He didn't steal the necklace, she did. She's the one who should be facing a prison sentence."

"If you know that for a fact," I said, "then why are you pressing the charge against him? Why not just drop it?"

Fleeting smile, small and mean. "She's the one who hid the necklace in his van, to save herself. And I intend to see that she pays for it, one way or another."

"Why do you hate her so much?"

"That's none of your business. You just go and tell her what I said."

"There wouldn't be any point in it. As I told you, Cory Beckett is no longer my client."

"Then what are you doing here, bothering me?"

I took a breath before I said, "Candidly, Mrs. Vorhees, it's because of an apparently legitimate concern for your welfare."

"My welfare?" Long, dark stare. "Are you threatening me?"

"Of course not. Exactly the opposite."

"The opposite of what? You're not making sense."

"Look, this isn't easy for me. I'm trying to explain the best way I know how. My associates and I have uncovered certain credible information that leads us to believe your life may be in danger. We felt it our duty to make you aware of the threat."

". . . That's a ridiculous statement."

"No, ma'am. It isn't."

"For God's sake! What information?"

"I can't tell you that. It's hearsay and we have no proof as yet to back it up."

"So you expect me to believe my life is in danger just because you say so? I don't know you. I don't know anything about you."

"I've been a detective for thirty years and my agency is considered one of the most reputable in the city. If you'd like a list of references —"

"Jesus," she said.

Then, abruptly, she stepped around me and went straight to the sideboard. Glass clinked against glass, no small amount of liquid gurgled. Whatever it was she poured, she tossed it off in a single flip of her wrist and backward toss of her head. She refilled the glass before she turned to face me again

— right up to the brim.

"In danger from whom?" she said, as if there had been no interruption in the conversation. "Not my husband, surely. He doesn't have the balls."

"I'm not in a position to tell you that."

"The Beckett whore, if I don't drop the charge against her brother?"

"I'm sorry — same answer."

"Damn you. You stand there claiming somebody wants me dead, but you won't say who or why."

I could feel my face heating up. This was going badly. I should have known it would; I should have stayed the hell away. "Legally and ethically, I can't make unsubstantiated accusations against anyone. All I can do —"

"Do you want money? Is that it?"

"No. All I can do is make you aware of the potential danger —"

"How much, goddamn you?"

"This isn't about money, Mrs. Vorhees. I'm just trying —"

"Oh, yes, sure. Just trying to be a good Samaritan. Well, that's a crock of you-know-what."

There was nothing I could say to that.

She knocked back half of her second drink, then came toward me again. Her face was splotchy now, the lipstick smeared; even in the pale lamplight I could see the anger like pinpoints of firelight in her eyes.

"Who?" she said in low, strained tones. "Who wants me dead?"

"I'm sorry, I can't give you any names."

"Names, plural. More than one person?"

I didn't say anything.

"The Beckett whore and who else? Her brother?"

"No."

"Damn you, then *who*?"

I could not just keep on standing there like a dummy. The urge to get the hell out was strong, but I'm not the kind of man who runs away from a difficult situation. All I could think was: She has a right to know, dammit. Give her something, let her figure it out for herself. But I knew I was making a mistake before all the words were out of my mouth.

"I'll say this much. When we were employed by Cory Beckett, there was a situation in which she brought along a friend to help her. A close friend, evidently, given the circumstances. His name is Frank Chaleen."

It rocked her. Her hand jerked enough to slop a little of the remaining whiskey over the rim of her glass.

"Frank? Frank and that slut? I don't believe it."

"The operative who was present can confirm it if you like."

"He's having an affair with her, too? She wants me dead and he's colluding with her? Is that what you're trying to tell me?"

"I've told you all I can, as much as I know to be fact."

"Meaning draw my own conclusions? Well, I won't draw them — I *don't* believe it." She looked half wild now, her face twisted out of shape. "You're a goddamn liar."

"No, ma'am, I'm not —"

"Liar! *Liar!*"

And all in one motion, with no warning, she threw the glass at me.

I was half-turning away from her and I didn't see it coming in time to dodge. The heavy crystal bottom edge slammed into my forehead, just above the bridge of my nose, with enough force to jerk loose a yelp of pain and knock me cock-eyed. I staggered backward, banged into an end table and sent an unlighted lamp crashing to the floor. I went down after it, hard on my side on the rough-weave carpet. My vision was still out of whack; I swiped a hand across my forehead, felt an open stinging gash and the stickiness of blood mixed with whiskey. The liquor stench made my gorge rise.

Dimly I heard the maid come running into the room, calling out querulously in Spanish. Margaret Vorhees told her to shut up, go get some towels, look at all that damn blood. The maid hesitated, said something about first aid; there was a brief argument, the words all jumbled together through a sharp buzzing in my ears. I twitched around on the floor, still trying to swipe my vision clear so that I could see. More sounds flowed around me, but no more voices, and when the room finally swam back into focus I saw that I was alone.

I shoved up onto my knees. My right hand was smeared with diluted blood; little streams of it spilling down around my nose kept trying to screw up my vision again. I caught hold of the table and hauled myself upright, but I had to keep leaning on it for support, woozy and wobbly, aware now of a blistering, throbbing pain across my forehead into both temples.

I was still standing there, trying to pull myself together, when the maid hurried back into the room. She made concerned noises at me in both English and Spanish, only some of which penetrated — asking if I was all right, if I needed a doctor. I managed to say yes and then no, and let her take my arm and guide me to one of the couches and sit me down. She'd brought a first-aid kit and an armload of wet towels; gently, she sopped up most of the blood around the wound and on the rest of my face, said something that sounded like "not too bad," and then went to work with an antiseptic that stung like hell and some gauze and adhesive tape.

By the time she was done, the dizziness and disorientation were gone and I was all right except for the headache. Margaret Vorhees hadn't put in an appearance, and wouldn't, but not because she was contrite or ashamed. She just didn't want anything more to do with me, with or without the blood. There was nothing I could do about the glass-throwing incident and she knew it. It was her house, I hadn't been invited, and I'd upset her with vague and unsubstantiated claims. The hell with me.

Yeah, and the hell with her, too.

I felt like the damn fool I was for coming here.

Pretty soon I tried standing up, and that was all right; then I tried walking a little and that was all right, too. The maid was down on her knees now, scrubbing at the spatters of blood and whiskey on the carpet — orders from Mrs. Vorhees, no doubt. She gave me a sad, sympathetic look underlain with something that might have been bitterness or exasperation, or maybe both. I thanked her in Spanish, and she said, *"De nada, por favor."* She would have dutifully gotten up to show me out if I hadn't made a stay-put gesture and told her I could find my own way.

Outside in the car, I peered at myself at the rearview mirror. Christ. The area around the bandaged wound was puffy and already starting to discolor. The maid had gotten most of the fluids off my face, but there were still spots and streaks here and there. On my shirt, tie, and jacket, too. It looked as though I'd been in a fight and gotten the worst of it. Hell of a time explaining this to Kerry, I thought, after my promise to keep myself out of harm's way.

But that concern became irrelevant in the next minute or so. It didn't matter what had just happened to me; it was simply no longer important.

I keep my cell phone turned off when I'm in somebody's home or office; I sat there a little longer to make sure I was okay to drive before it occurred to me to check for messages. There was one on my voice mail, from Kerry. A message that slammed me harder and did more damage than Margaret Vorhees' crystal tumbler; that really ripped the day apart, turned it dark and bleak and far more painful.

"The on-duty doctor at Redwood Village just called," she said. Very calm, very controlled, as if she were holding herself in rigid check. "Cybil had a massive stroke this morning. She died before they could move her from the clinic to the hospital."

12

TAMARA

The first time the guy called asking for Bill, she had no idea who he was. Just an unfamiliar voice on the phone, kind of tight and demanding. She told him Bill wasn't there and probably wouldn't be available the rest of the week. He said, "I have to see him," and she said, "I'm sorry, that's not possible, may I take a message?" No message. Was there something she could help him with? Evidently not. He hung up on her without giving his name.

The second call came a few minutes later, while she was taking a short break to drink her second cup of coffee and brood a little. About Bill and Kerry and the death of Kerry's mother, mainly. He'd called her with the news last night. She had never met Cybil Wade, but she knew how close Kerry and her mother were from the things Bill had told her. She felt bad for both of them. Old people died every day and Cybil Wade had had a good, long life, but that didn't make it any easier for her family to deal with.

Man, they'd had so much crap in their lives, Kerry especially the past couple of years, and now this. Wasn't right that bad things kept happening to good people while the bastards in the world went right on sailing along on untroubled seas.

Thinking the word "bastard" led her straight to thinking about Horace again, like continually picking at a splinter or a scab. He wasn't one of the worst, but he still ran with the pack. Damn the man! She couldn't make up her mind what to do about him.

Why hadn't he stayed in Philadelphia instead of coming home to the city and slithering back into her life? Well, she didn't have to have let him, never mind how contrite he was or pretended to be. Didn't have to start sleeping with him again, either, for God's sake. What a weak, stupid mistake *that'd* been! Same old silver-tongue Horace, talk the panties right off a girl even after she vowed not to let it happen.

Never mind, either, that he was still the best lover she'd ever had, maybe the best she would ever have. It was just sex now, wasn't it? Sure it was; she didn't love him anymore, not the way she had before he dumped her for another cellist in the Philadelphia orchestra. Served him right that Mary from Rochester dumped him for some other guy after he'd gone and put a ring on her finger.

Sex, no matter how good . . . well, it just wasn't as important as it had been when she was living with him. She was older now, smarter (most of the time, anyway), she had responsibilities and a job she loved, she didn't need or want Horace complicating her life and maybe messing it up again. She'd told him that, and he swore he'd never hurt her again, he was a changed man. Maybe fact, maybe bullshit. Whatever, he wouldn't go away and leave her be. And she couldn't seem to just say no, just tell him adios, and lock the doors every time he came sucking around. . . .

This was what was going through her mind when the phone rang and the same dude as before started another rap about needing to see Bill ASAP. He sounded even more tight-assed this time, as if he were upset about something and working to keep himself under control.

"Where is he? Not in the hospital, is he?"

"The hospital? No. Why would you think that?"

"Out of town, then, or what?"

"I can't tell you that. What's your business with him?"

"That's between him and me. Can you get a message to him? Have him get in touch with me right away? Not by phone, in person."

"I might be able to, if it's important enough."

"It's important, all right."

"Who am I talking to?"

Long pause before he countered with, "Who're you?"

"Tamara Corbin. Partner in this agency."

"Partner." Another pause. "This is Frank Chaleen."

Tamara wasn't surprised. The hospital question had tipped her. The other thing Bill had told her last night was a brief account of how Margaret Vorhees had tried to brain him with a whiskey glass.

She said, playing the dude, "What was that name again?"

"Frank Chaleen. You know who I am."

"Do I? What makes you think so?"

Pause number three. Then, "Don't you people talk to each other?"

"Usually. When there's good reason."

"Your partner didn't say anything to you about me?"

"I didn't say that. How do I know you're

who you claim to be? Just a voice on the telephone."

Chaleen didn't like that. She could tell she'd gotten under his skin; his voice had an angry wobble when he said, "You get a message to him, tell him to come talk to me." He rapped out the address of Chaleen Manufacturing. "Tell him he'd better show up soon if he knows what's good for him."

Like hell I will, Tamara thought. She said, "Good-bye, Mr. Careen," deliberately mispronouncing his name, and hung up on him this time.

Jake Runyon came in a little before one. She was expecting him; he'd been in the city all morning, finishing up a hit-and-run investigation for the victim's attorney, and had told her yesterday that he'd stop in with a report and to see if she had anything new for him.

She let him get his business out of the way first. Pulled up the hit-and-run casefile and made notes on it while he talked, in between bites from the sandwich she'd brought from home. When he was done, she said, "News, Jake, none of it good," and told him, first, about Cybil Wade dying. She'd thought about notifying him last night after Bill's call, but why lay a load of gloom on the man

137

after he'd put in a long day on and off the road? There was nothing he could do. Nothing she could do, either.

Jake had one of these immobile faces that seldom showed emotion, made it hard to guess what he was thinking. Not so much now, though. The news had the same effect on him that it had had on her. The way one side of his mouth twitched and he muttered, "Damn," told her that.

"Bill said Kerry seems to be coping all right so far, but after all she's been through . . ."

"Yeah."

"Be a while before he comes back to work. So we'll have to take up the slack, maybe put in even more overtime."

"That's no problem."

Tamara said, "He got the news just after talking to Margaret Vorhees yesterday. That went down hard for him, too."

"What happened?"

"She was drunk, belligerent. Wouldn't believe she was in any danger. He told her as much as he could . . . a little too much, maybe, he said. Dropped Chaleen's name, intimated Cory Beckett was screwing him as well as her husband, and she went ballistic. Called him a liar, threw a glass at him that he didn't see coming in time to duck."

"He all right?"

"Cut on the forehead, otherwise okay," Tamara said. "But he must've got through to her despite the tantrum. Enough for her to yank Chaleen's chain and put him in a snit."

"How do you know that?"

"Man called up twice this morning, looking for Bill. Must be real anxious to know how Bill found out enough about him and the Beckett bitch to warn Mrs. Vorhees."

"What did you tell him?"

"Put him off for the time being. He didn't like it, made a half-assed threat against Bill."

"Worried. Nervous, if not scared."

"Right. But worried enough to call off whatever they're planning?"

"If they think Bill knows too much about it."

"His idea or hers for Chaleen to talk to him, try to find out?"

"His," Jake said. "He may not even have told her about Bill's warning. Waiting to get more information first."

"She's the one pulling the strings."

"So it would seem."

"Anyhow," Tamara said, "Bill stirred things up pretty good yesterday. What do you think of stirring 'em up a little more?"

"What do you have in mind?"

"You go see Chaleen instead. Walk in on him cold, let on you know what Bill knows without saying what it is. Same careful approach he took with Mrs. Vorhees."

Jake thought it over. "Tricky," he said. "And it means getting in deeper than we already are. We're putting a lot of faith in an emotionally damaged kid's story as it is."

"You still believe Kenny told you the truth?"

"The truth as he perceives it, yes."

"Doubts, Jake? Second thoughts?"

"About some of the details, maybe."

"But not about the gun?"

"No. Cory's got one, all right."

"And not that there's a murder scheme?"

"My gut feeling says Beckett's right about that."

"So if you talk to Chaleen," Tamara said, "and come on strong enough, you might be able to shake him up enough so he backs out on Cory. No murder scheme without him, right?"

"Theoretically."

"It's worth a shot. Okay?"

"Okay."

Tamara said, "Just watch out he doesn't get pissed enough to chuck something at your head. And make sure you duck in time if he does."

13

JAKE RUNYON

Frank Chaleen's factory was on Basin Street, on the southeastern side of the city near the Islais Creek Channel. Basin ran at an angle off Evans: four blocks long and lined with small factories and warehousing companies, an auto-body shop, an outfit that made statuary for gardens and cemeteries, and midway along the last block, a pair of buildings crowded behind a chain-link fence topped by strands of barbed wire. Signs on the fence and on the largest of the two buildings identified the place as Chaleen Manufacturing, Inc.

The main structure was an L-shaped hunk of rust-spotted corrugated iron; a much smaller building, a squat trailer-like affair that sat behind and to one side like a broken-off piece of the factory, figured to be the office. Both buildings had a neglected look, not quite rundown yet but getting to that point. There were two double gates in the fence — truck-wide and standing open — that gave access to a trio of bays in the facing factory wall, one of the bays filled by a semi being loaded or unloaded. The asphalt yard needed resurfacing: cracked, pitted, buckled in a couple of places.

Another set of gates, farther along and smaller, provided direct access to the trailer-like structure. Runyon pulled up near these. They, too, were open; he walked on through and up to the office entrance. A promotional poster headed WE'RE ECO-FRIENDLY! was pinned to the door; words underneath proclaimed that Chaleen's X-Cel Packing Peanuts were non-toxic, reusable, biodegradable in compost, and dissolvable in water. One of the poster's corners had come loose, some time ago judging from the way it was curled up.

Runyon stepped inside. The interior appeared to have been cut into two more or less equal halves by a center wall. Four desks, only one of them occupied, were jammed into the near half. In the bisecting wall were two closed and unmarked doors, one of which would probably lead to private quarters in the rear half.

Runyon told the lone employee, a young dark-haired woman wearing a pair of red-rimmed glasses, that he was there to see Frank Chaleen. She said, "Mr. Chaleen is out in the factory. He should be back shortly. If you'd like to wait . . ."

"I'll just wander over there, if there's no rule against visitors."

"Well, no, there isn't, but —"

"He's anxious to see me. Whereabouts in the factory?"

"The manufacturing section. One of our extrusion machines has broken down again. He went over there to look at it."

Extrusion machine. Whatever that was.

Runyon thanked her, walked out and across the yard to a set of cracked concrete steps that led up onto the loading dock. A warehouseman driving a forklift was loading a pallet laden with cardboard drums into the maw of the semi parked in the nearest bay; he didn't seem to be working too hard at it. He paid no attention as Runyon entered the warehouse, a cavernous, fluorescent-lighted space crowded with more of the drums, as well as stacks of cardboard cartons and bundled plastic bags.

Only one man was working in there, checking off items on a clipboard. He had no interest in Runyon, either. The clatter and hum of machinery coming from beyond the open inner end drew Runyon into the factory proper. The complicated maze of manufacturing equipment in there meant nothing to him; he focused on a group of men in front of a machine that wasn't making any noise, two of them in overalls working on it with hand tools, the other two standing by watching. One of the watchers, wearing a shirt and tie but no jacket, was Frank Chaleen.

Chaleen didn't see Runyon until he came right up next to him. First reaction: a frown. Then, on recognition: a small double take followed by a scowl and a slitty-eyed stare. Neither of them said anything for five or six beats. Then Chaleen turned to the foreman, saying, "I'll be right back, Ed," and moved away in hard strides, Runyon following.

Chaleen stopped abruptly at the warehouse entrance, turned, resumed the hard-eyed glare. "What the hell are you doing here?"

"You wanted to talk to my boss; he's not available. So you get me instead."

"I don't have anything to say to you."

"Not even if I know what he knows?"

The muscle quirk at the corner of Chaleen's mouth twitched it open on that side, curling the upper lip and revealing a canine tooth — an expression like a dog's silent snarl. As much a nervous reaction as one of either belligerence or anger.

"Knows about what?"

"What you wanted to talk to him about."

"Don't play games with me, man. I don't like it."

Runyon said, "Margaret Vorhees."

"Well? What about her?"

"She told you about his visit to her yesterday."

"So? What if she did? He gave her a load of crap about Cory Beckett and me being out to get her."

"That's not what he said. He didn't make any accusations against either of you."

"How do you know? You weren't there."

"He doesn't operate that way. All he tried to do was make Mrs. Vorhees aware of a potentially volatile situation."

"Volatile, my ass. I ought to sue the son of a bitch for slander."

"Waste of time and money," Runyon said. "We both know you don't have grounds."

Chaleen made a fist of one hand, but it wasn't meant as a threat; he banged the fist against his thigh before allowing the fingers to relax. "Margaret doesn't have anything to fear from me," he said. "From that asshole she's married to, maybe, but not from me."

"Nothing to fear from Cory Beckett, either?"

"Hell, no. Why would Cory want to harm her?"

"The diamond necklace her brother allegedly stole. Mrs. Vorhees refuses to drop the charges."

"I know that. So what? Cory says the kid didn't steal it. Her lawyer'll get him off."

"The two of you seem to be pretty close."

"Wrong. Casual acquaintances, that's all."

"You were with her when she picked up her brother at Belardi's."

"Don't try to make anything out of that. I wasn't the first person she called that day."

Runyon didn't say anything.

"Listen," Chaleen said, "there's nothing going on with Cory and me. I haven't even seen or talked to her since."

"Not even to tell her about my boss's visit to Mrs. Vorhees?"

"Hell, no. Why should I bother her with his crap?"

Nothing to say to that, either.

"Crazy notion that the two us have it in for Margaret. Where'd your boss get it, anyway? You the one put a bug in his ear?"

"Where would I get a bug like that?"

"How the hell do I know?" Pause. Then the mouth corner twisted up again. "Unless

146

somebody put a bug in yours."

"Somebody like who?"

"Her screwed-up brother. Yeah, sure, that's it. Kenny. You spent a lot of time with him up there at the river."

Runyon didn't like lying, but it was called for here. "We didn't talk much. Nothing was said about you and his sister."

"No? Maybe he got in touch with you later. Told you a pack of lies."

"Why would he do that?"

"Because he doesn't like me. Because he's got a few screws loose. Cory says he makes up stories all the time."

"I haven't seen or talked to Kenneth Beckett since Belardi's," Runyon lied again. "I don't know anything about his mental state. But you seem to know him pretty well."

"Well enough to tell he's a sick kid. Druggie, too. Addicted to amphetamines."

"So his sister claims, but he wasn't high when I found him. And I didn't find any evidence of drugs in the shack or his van."

"So maybe he used up his supply," Chaleen said. "How would you know if he was stoned or not? You're no damn doctor."

Runyon let that go. "Have you ever seen him stoned?"

"Couple of times, yeah."

147

"So then you must have spent a fair amount of time with him and his sister."

"Goddamn it! I told you, Cory's just a friend. Get that through your head. Nothing more than a casual friend."

"Like Margaret Vorhees is a casual friend?"

"Now what the hell are you insinuating?"

"I'm not insinuating anything. Just going on what seems to be common knowledge."

"About Margaret and me? Malicious gossip. There's nothing between us, any more than there is between Cory and me."

"Cory and Andrew Vorhees," Runyon said. "Is that just malicious gossip, too?"

Push enough buttons and you're bound to hit an unprotected sensitive spot. Chaleen's face went dirty with a surge of anger. He took a half step forward, his hand lifting and fisting again. "I've had enough of you and your bullshit, man. I ought to break your face."

Runyon hadn't moved. "Welcome to try. But don't forget what happened at Belardi's."

Chaleen hadn't forgotten. He might have tried to get physical with somebody else, but when you can't back a man down with threats, you're vulnerable and already half beaten. He knew it, knew what the result would be if he forced the issue; it frustrated him, but it also made him afraid. As before, as always when he came up against a man like Runyon, he was the one who backed down.

His fingers relaxed again, his gaze slid away. Then, "You're trespassing. Get out of here before I call the cops and have you arrested!" The last sentence came out loud enough so that the warehouseman with the clipboard turned to look at them.

Runyon said slowly, in a voice that didn't carry, "And don't forget this conversation, or the one my boss had yesterday with Mrs. Vorhees."

Red-faced, Chaleen shouted again. "You people go around making any more veiled accusations against me, you'll hear from my lawyer! You got that? All right, now get the hell out!"

Runyon went, taking his time, not looking back.

In the Ford, before he drove away from Chaleen Manufacturing, he reported in to Tamara.

"So you think you scared him off?" she asked.

"Hard to tell. Maybe, maybe not."

"Man'd have to have his head up his butt

to try anything now, knowing we're onto him."

"You'd think so," Runyon said. "He claimed he didn't tell Cory about Bill's talk with Margaret Vorhees. That might be the truth."

"Why wouldn't he have told her?"

"Afraid of her reaction, maybe. He may have already had second thoughts about going through with their plan."

"I wouldn't put it past her to go ahead with or without him," Tamara said, "if the plan's good enough and the stakes big enough. Everything in her record says she's an aggressive risk taker."

"But not unless she figures it's a sure thing. If she does go ahead, it won't be alone."

"Right. Not the type to do her own dirty work. So then she'll need Chaleen."

Runyon said, "And she'll make every effort to get him to do what she wants. Whether or not she succeeds depends on how strong her hold on him is. And on what else is in it for him."

"You mean money?"

"If there's enough to be had. That factory of his isn't doing too well. Skeletal crew, machinery breaking down, buildings and property in disrepair."

"So he could be heavy in debt," Tamara said. "I'll run a financial check on him — should've thought to do that before." Then, after a pause, "What do you think about having a talk with Cory, Jake? Would it do any good?"

Runyon said, "No. Kenneth's on thin ice as it is. Chaleen picked up on the idea he's the one who tipped us. I think I talked him out of it, but she's smarter than he is."

"Yeah. Well, what about trying to get Kenny alone for another talk?"

"Same objection. Too much chance of Cory catching wise. There's nothing he can do to diffuse the situation. If he tries, he's liable to make it worse."

"So we've done all we can and we're back to square one. Just wait and hope nothing happens."

"I don't see any other alternative," Runyon said.

14

Any sudden death in the family is a blow, and when the person is as close as Cybil was to us it's twice as hard to deal with, twice as painful. Never mind that she had been in her late eighties and in failing health, and you knew her time was short and you'd resigned yourself to the inevitable loss. When it happens it's still unexpected, a shock you don't easily recover from.

Bad enough for Emily and me; devastating for Kerry. Her mother had been a vital presence in her life — confidante, touchstone, tower of strength in times of crisis. Cybil's passing must have torn her up inside, and yet she coped with it — or seemed to be coping with it — in the same calm, controlled way she'd broken the news to me. No outward displays of emotion; if she cried, and she surely must have, it was in private behind locked doors. She comforted Emily when the girl burst into tears after being told. She let both of us try to comfort her with hugs and inadequate words, but not for any length of time and with a kind of mild but distant reserve.

The only indication of the depth of her grief was when she and I were in bed the night it happened, a few whispered words in the darkness. "What hurts the most," she said, "was that I couldn't be with her at the end. To tell her how much I loved her. To say good-bye."

There was no funeral or memorial service, at Cybil's request. She had asked to be cremated and to have her ashes scattered in Muir Woods, one of her favorite places. Kerry insisted on taking care of the mortuary arrangements herself. She also insisted on immediately clearing out her mother's unit at Redwood Village in Larkspur.

"There's no reason to wait," she said. She also said, "It doesn't seem right for all her things to be sitting there gathering dust now that she's gone."

She let me help her do the clearing and gathering, but I suspected it was only because she couldn't manage the task alone. Cybil's personal possessions were relatively few: a small trunk full of old correspondence, photographs, clippings of news items and book reviews, miscellaneous scraps of paper, and carbon-copy manuscripts of the stories she'd written under the pseudonym Samuel Leatherman for *Black Mask, Dime Detective,* and *Midnight Detective* in the 1940s; several framed family photos, a few mementoes and knick-knacks; and two boxes of books and magazines, including extra copies of *Dead Eye* and *Black Eye,* Cybil's two retro novels featuring her hard-boiled pulp detective, Max Ruffe.

Kerry wanted all of this transported to our condo, along with her mother's ancient Remington typewriter and antique rocking chair, the small bookcase in which the copies of Cybil's published works had been displayed, and a couple of items of clothing that had some sort of sentimental value. "All of these were part of Cybil, dear to her. How can I get rid of them?" She said this defensively, even though I hadn't questioned her or made any kind of comment.

When we were done, the only things left for Redwood Village to dispose of were the remaining items of furniture, cookware and glassware, and the contents of the refrigerator and cupboards. It took both Kerry's car and mine to get all the stuff back to the city.

Once we had everything inside the condo, all but filling up the utility room, she began sorting through the contents of the trunk — a task she wouldn't let me help her with. "It's my job. Most of these things are personal."

"I won't look at anything you don't want me to."

"That's not the point. I don't want any help."

"Kerry, I know how much you're hurting —"

"Do you?"

"All right, maybe not, but Cybil's passing deeply affected me, too —"

"Passing," Kerry said between her teeth. "God, you know I hate that euphemism. Cybil died. My mother *died*."

"Her death, then. I'm just trying to make things a little easier for you, that's all."

"Then don't fuss and let me do what I have to do."

I did not put up any further argument.

Kerry spent that evening and part of the next morning going through the trunk and the boxes of books. Looking at photographs, reading correspondence or part of a manuscript or a story in one of the pulp magazines or one of the dozens of yellowed pieces of paper on which Cybil had scribbled story ideas, character sketches, sentence fragments. One of the times I wandered in to see how she was doing, I found her stroking with her index finger a small stone carving of a panther that Cybil had kept on the bureau in her bedroom.

"My father gave this to her on her fortieth birthday."

"What's it carved from?" I asked. "Onyx?"

"Black jade. From Burma. He said it had magical powers."

"She never mentioned that."

"She didn't believe it. Neither do I."

"But he did?"

"He claimed he did. I'm not so sure he believed in any of that occult crap he wrote about."

Telling statement. Ivan Wade had started out as a pulp writer himself, concocting grim and gruesome stories for *Weird Tales* and other fantasy/horror magazines, and then had gravitated to radio scripting, slick magazine fiction, some TV work, and finally novels and nonfiction books on occult and magic themes. Kerry adored Cybil's work, but hadn't much cared for any of her father's — an accurate reflection of her feelings toward her parents as individuals. Cybil had been warm and nurturing, Ivan cold and distant. I'd met him at the same pulp convention in San Francisco where I'd first met Kerry and Cybil, and disliked him intensely; he'd been nasty as hell to me, tried to keep Kerry and me apart on the claim that I was too old for her and in too dangerous a profession. Kerry had loved him, but she hadn't mourned his death several years ago half as much as she was mourning Cybil's.

When she was finally done with the sorting, she carefully restored every photograph and scrap of paper to the trunk and then asked me to move it into her office. She'd have liked the bookcase and rocking chair in there, too, but there wasn't enough room for both; as it was I had to shift some of the existing furniture around to make the bookcase fit. She settled for putting the rocker in a corner of the living room.

From memory she filled the bookcase with Cybil's published works in the exact order they'd been in her mother's apartment, and had me take the remaining books down to our basement storage unit. Then she placed the typewriter, some of the saved gewgaws, and most of the framed photographs on top. The rest of the curios and framed photos, including a prominent one of Cybil in her midthirties at her typewriter, ended up on Kerry's already cluttered desk.

A shrine. That was the overall effect, and

her intention whether a conscious one or not.

Neither Emily nor I said anything about it. What can you say to a grieving and emotionally fragile woman in circumstances like these? Nothing meaningful or worthwhile. If Kerry needed a shrine to help her cope, then that was fine with us. I'd have turned the whole flat into one if that was what it took to help her get through this new crisis.

What worried me was that her control was mostly surface; that once the necessities had been dealt with and the shrine was in place she would begin to withdraw again into that dark corner of herself where she'd huddled for the weeks after the Green Valley ordeal. Recurring nightmares, not wanting to be touched, weight loss, refusal to leave the flat alone and then only with me for visits to her doctor or with Cybil. I was afraid for her, and afraid that neither Emily nor I was equipped to handle it if it happened again. The stress and emotional drain of those weeks had taken their toll on us as well as on Kerry.

I had a private talk with Emily on the subject — she's far more mature than her fourteen years — and she agreed that we would have to once again adopt the same careful mode as before. Be there for Kerry when she needed us, but put no pressure on her of any kind. Maintain as much of a normal home environment as we could at all times.

But it seemed that our fears were groundless. For the time being, at least.

On the morning of the third day after Cybil's death, Kerry went back to her office at Bates and Carpenter. There was a lot of work piled up on her desk, she said, and a client conference that she felt obligated to attend. A healthy decision, as far as I was concerned; I'd thought she might opt for holing up in her condo office and working from home by telephone and computer, as she had during her long recuperation. She was still a little distant with Emily and me, unwilling to share more than little pieces of her grief. Throwing herself into her work might be just what was needed to reestablish her equilibrium and the equanimity of our home life.

With Emily back in school, I did not have much reason to hang around the flat, either. The wound Margaret Vorhees had inflicted on my forehead was not severe enough to require stitches. I didn't think so, anyway, after I'd removed the bandage the Latina maid had put on and in the bathroom mirror inspected the gash and a purplish bruise that haloed it. Nor did Emily, who insisted on an inspection of her own and then applied more antiseptic and a fresh bandage. Not Kerry, though. She didn't ask me what had happened until the morning after Cybil's death; the bandage and bruise may not have even registered until then. I made light of both the incident and the wound and she took me at my word, let the subject drop without question.

I'd worried a little about the possibility of a concussion because my headache had lingered overnight and bothered me while Kerry and I were loading and unloading Cybil's possessions, but it was gone by that evening; and I hadn't had any other symptoms. The gouge was deep enough to leave a very small scar, maybe, without a doctor's attention and a couple of stitches, but that prospect bothered me not at all. What was one more scar among the many?

So I went back to work myself, at least for that day. Routine desk work, same as before. I'd been in touch with Tamara, of course, and Jake Runyon had called to offer his condolences. They had filled me in on Jake's face-to-face with Frank Chaleen. Nothing had happened since. The waiting game was still in effect.

But something was going to happen sooner or later. Probably sooner, since Kenneth Beckett's trial was rapidly approaching. We all pretty much agreed on that. This was one of those powderkeg cases, with all the principals and their interactions so unstable that an explosion of some kind seemed inevitable. What worried me was that when it came, one or more of us would suffer collateral damage a lot worse than a cut on the forehead.

15

JAKE RUNYON

Seven-fifteen p.m., the following Wednesday.

Runyon had just come out of a Chinese restaurant on Taraval, a few blocks from his apartment. Chinese food had been Colleen's favorite; they'd eaten one kind or another two or three times a week during their twenty years together. After she was gone he'd kept up the ritual as a way to hold onto the memory of the good times they'd shared. But during his period with Bryn, he ate Chinese less often and only on nights when he was alone. Now he was back to it regularly again, but not in a compulsive way. Because as much as he cared for any food, he liked Hunan and Szechuan. And because every time he ordered a plate of moo shu pork or sesame chicken, he visualized Colleen's smile and felt her there close to him once again.

He was keying open the door to his Ford

when his cell vibrated. The caller window told him who it was.

Kenneth Beckett. Finally.

He slid in behind the wheel before he opened the line. "Yes, Ken?"

"Oh man I'm glad you picked up, I can't talk very long." Fast, breathless, the kid's voice pitched low; Runyon had to strain a little to hear him. "Cory's in the shower and Mr. Vorhees will be here any minute. It's tonight, Mr. Runyon, he's going to do it tonight."

"Who is? Do what?"

"Chaleen. Kill Mrs. Vorhees."

"How do you know that?"

"The way Cory's been acting, all excited, going out to meet that bastard . . . I know it's tonight. I'd've called sooner but this is the first chance I've had. You've got to stop him."

"Where? How?"

"I don't know."

"What makes you so sure it's Chaleen and not both of them?"

"Cory never does anything herself, she always makes other people do what she wants. She —"

Audible in the background was a sudden chiming noise. Doorbell.

"Oh God, Mr. Vorhees is here," Beckett

whispered. Panicky now. "Don't let Chaleen do it, Mr. Runyon, don't let her be killed!"

"Ken, wait —"

The line went dead.

A light fog was drifting in from the ocean, just thick enough to wrap the tops of trees in faintly luminous skeins, as Runyon drove into St. Francis Wood. He had a good memory for addresses; he'd remembered the street and number of the Vorhees home without having to look them up. He swung off Sloat below the fountain at the boulevard's upper end, rolled slowly along the cross street to the big Spanish-style house. Even with all the vegetation, he could see that the porch light was on and that another burned behind one of the thinly curtained front windows. Security lights, possibly, but he wouldn't know for sure until he checked. He parked just beyond the driveway.

The mist made the evening chilly; he pulled his coat collar up as he passed through a gate in the front hedge. Risky business, coming here. For all he knew, Beckett had made up or imagined an attack tonight on Margaret Vorhees. But he couldn't afford to ignore the possibility that the kid was right and something was about to go down.

This was the only place he knew to start looking for Margaret Vorhees. If she was home alone, he'd have to make up some kind of story for the after-dark visit, one that wouldn't provoke the kind of alcoholic rage she'd directed at Bill. If Chaleen was there and she was all right, he'd still have to make up a story, but his arrival ought to be enough to prevent her from being harmed. Temporarily, anyhow.

Moot concerns: nobody answered the bell.

The house's security system wasn't armed; the red light on the alarm panel would have been on if it was. Still possible she was here, then, drunk and not answering the bell. He rang it again — four, five, six times. Chimes, fading echoes, silence.

Runyon tried the latch. Locked. Just as well; he had no cause for an illegal entry.

He turned back down off the porch. Thinking: Check the detached garage, see if he could tell if her car was inside. He'd have a choice to make if it wasn't, and neither of the options worth a damn. Hunting for the woman was needle-in-a-haystack stuff. Waiting here for her to come home was potentially just as futile; if Beckett was right and she'd gone to meet Chaleen, she wouldn't be coming home at all.

A flagstone path led to the garage through a geometrical arrangement of flower beds and thick, tall shrubbery; outdoor lantern-style lights were strung along it, but they were all dark. He picked his way to where the path angled around some kind of flowering shrub, and then he could see the garage and a lighted window in the nearside wall. The interior overheads left on for some reason?

The path angled toward the window and a closed side door beyond. As he drew closer, he realized that the light behind the glass had an oddly unsteady, nebulous quality. That was the first warning sign. The others came quickly: a low, steady rumbling from inside the garage, just audible in the night's stillness, then a faint acrid smell that twitched his nostrils — familiar, too familiar.

Runyon broke into a run, the skin pulling along the back of his neck. When he put his face up close to the window, he was looking at moving layers of gray as if thick clouds of fog had been trapped inside. Through the billows he could make out the shape of a low-slung sports car, its engine throbbing like an erratic pulse.

The door next to the window was locked or jammed. Runyon ran around to the front, but there were no outside handles on the double garage doors: electronically controlled and locked down tight. Back fast to the window in the sidewall, where he broke the glass with his elbow. The construction of the garage must have provided a tight seal; waves of carbon monoxide came pouring out, driving him back and to one side.

He ducked his head, threw his weight against the door, but he couldn't break through that way, succeeded only in jamming his shoulder. Then he did what he should have done in the first place — stepped back, pistoned the bottom of his shoe into the panel next to the knob. The second time he did that, the lock tore loose and the door scraped inward on the concrete floor.

Runyon shoved it all the way open, releasing more of the churning poison, held a sucked-in breath, and plunged blindly inside.

Despite the dull furry glow from an overhead light, he could barely see; the monoxide burned his eyes, started them stinging and watering. He smacked into the car on the passenger side, bent to squint through the window. A figure was slumped over the wheel, but he couldn't make out whether it was a man or a woman. He fumbled for the door handle. Locked. Clawed his way around to the driver's side. That door was locked, too.

The exhaust fumes had gotten into his lungs, was tearing the air out of them in a burst of staccato coughing. No way he could stay in here now without putting himself at risk. He groped back around the car, stumbled out through the side door. Leaned against the garage wall, gulping fog-damp air until his head and chest cleared.

When he could breathe again, he dragged out his pencil flash and ran along the path to the house to hunt for a hose bib. Found one, soaked his handkerchief in cold water. The emissions were no longer quite as thick when he returned to the garage; he could see the car more clearly now, a black Mercedes. He sucked in another breath, held the wet handkerchief over his mouth and nose, pushed back inside.

First thing was to get the double entrance doors open to let more of the monoxide empty out. He no longer felt any sense of urgency; as dense as the trapped fumes had been, the Mercedes' engine had to've been running a long time — much too long for the person slumped behind the wheel to still be alive. He splashed the walls with pen light until he located the switch that operated the automatic door opener. When the mechanism began to grind, he turned back toward a work-bench that stretched along one wall.

A bunch of hand tools hung neatly on a pegboard. Hammer . . . no, it'd take too long to break through safety glass on a Mercedes. Pry bar was what he needed. There, hanging behind a handsaw. He yanked it down.

Coughing again, he managed to wedge the thin end of the bar into the crack next to the lock on the driver's door. Couldn't spring it at first, thought he'd have to use the bar to beat a hole in the glass, then gave it one more yank and the door popped open.

He threw the bar down, leaned in past the slumped figure — a woman — and twisted the ignition key to cut off the wheezing rhythm of the engine. The woman and the car interior both stank of whiskey. He got both hands under her arms, dragged her limp body out of the car. His legs had a rubbery feel by the time he'd hauled her partway down the driveway; the drop to his knees beside her was as much a temporary collapse as a willful lowering. His chest still burned, sickness roiled in his stomach.

Somebody started shouting out on the

street, but Runyon was too focused on the woman to pay much attention. Fortyish, black hair piled atop her head, eyes wide open with the whites showing, lips stretched wide and curled inward, the skin of her face a bright cherry red. No need to feel for a pulse, but he did it anyway. Too late, much too late. Would've been too late even if he'd gotten here twenty or thirty minutes sooner.

He had never seen Margaret Vorhees, but there was no doubt that she was the dead woman. He didn't need Bill's description of her to confirm it.

Running footsteps, two shouting voices now, a man and a woman. Neighbors. The man made a 911 call on his cell phone, and a good thing he was there to do it. Runyon didn't have enough breath left to speak above a cough-riddled whisper.

He was all right again by the time the police and an EMT unit showed up, but the EMTs insisted on checking him over and giving him oxygen. Then there was the usual q. & a. with a pair of patrolmen, and another round of the same with an African American homicide inspector named Samuel Davidson.

Why was Runyon there? A business matter to discuss with Mrs. Vorhees. What sort of business matter? Information the agency he worked for had come by pertaining to the theft of a valuable necklace of hers. Did he know the woman? No, he'd never seen her before. Was she a client of the agency? No. The information had come into their possession through another case they were investigating. Could the case have any connection with her death? He didn't know, couldn't say.

After that, Runyon faded into the background while the forensics and coroner's people went about their work. On the front seat of the Mercedes they found Margaret Vorhees' purse, the remote control unit that operated the garage doors, and a nearly empty bottle of Irish whiskey. According to the neighbors, Mrs. Vorhees had been drinking heavily since the separation from her husband. That opened up the possibility that she'd been despondent enough to take her own life, except that the police didn't find anything resembling a suicide note in the car or in the house. Which left the natural assumption that her death had been accidental. Alcoholic drives home from somewhere drunk, taking little nips of Irish on the way; pulls the car into the garage, presses the remote to lower the doors, then passes out with the engine still running.

Stupid, tragic accident. Happens all the time.

But not this time.

It was murder, all right.

Runyon would have figured it that way even if Kenneth Beckett hadn't put the bug in his ear. The monoxide job had a staged feel. The nearly empty whiskey bottle on the front seat was too convenient; well-bred socialites, no matter how alcoholic, were much less inclined to suck on an open bottle while driving than your average drunk. Then there were the overhead lights in the garage; if she'd been out somewhere in her Mercedes, why would she have left the lights burning? And the security system had been switched off. No wealthy woman living alone is likely to forget to arm hers when she leaves the house, no matter how much she's had to drink.

None of the neighbors the police talked to had noticed anyone in the vicinity during the afternoon. Even if they had seen a man who'd probably been an occasional if not frequent visitor, it wouldn't seem suspicious. And it would have been easy enough for that man to get Margaret Vorhees drunk enough to pass out, carry her through the jungley side yard to the garage, put her into the Mercedes along with the props, start the engine, set the snap lock on the side garage door, and then slip away unseen.

Frank Chaleen.

Working from a scheme designed by Cory Beckett.

It galled Runyon, believing this, to have to tell evasive half-truths to the law. But he was hamstrung. Even if he'd given Inspector Davidson Kenneth Beckett's name, chances were the kid would be too scared or too intimidated to corroborate his story of a murder plot. And if he did corroborate it, it would be the ragged hearsay testimony of an unstable young man awaiting trial for grand theft, against the words of his sister and a prominent businessman.

Another thing: you learned to tread cautiously with the law when you were working the private sector, if you wanted to keep your license. Cops liked cooperation, but what they didn't like were insupportable complications; Runyon was well aware of that from his time on the job in Seattle. In a case like this, the smart thing was to keep your mouth shut and let the investigating officers come to their own conclusions.

But even with the victim a prominent member of society, their investigation was likely to be superficial. Andrew Vorhees had a considerable amount of clout, and unless he had good reason to suspect foul play, he'd want the case closed quickly and with the least amount of publicity. The final verdict, in all likelihood, would be accidental death.

Which meant that unless Kenneth Beckett could be talked into testifying against his sister, she and Frank Chaleen would get away with cold-blooded murder.

16

Tamara, Runyon, and I held an early conference in her office the following morning. After hearing Jake's account of Margaret Vorhees' death — he'd notified us both after the police let him leave St. Francis Wood — it seemed pretty clear what Cory Beckett's motives were; we all agreed on that. Payback for the attempted frame-up was part of it, but the primary motive had to be greed: with the present Mrs. Vorhees out of the way, Cory had a clear shot at becoming the next in line. Marrying fat cats, as Tamara pointed out, had been her deal all along.

At first consideration, it seemed incredible that the murder plan had been carried out only two days after Runyon had confronted Frank Chaleen. But the more you considered the principals and the issues involved, the less untenable it seemed. Cory Beckett was whip-smart, bold, relentless, deadly clever, a brilliant manipulator of men, and at least a borderline psychotic — certainly unbalanced enough to consider herself invincible. She would not have gone ahead if she hadn't believed they would get away with it.

Timing was the primary reason: Margaret Vorhees had to die before her brother's trial. Once the woman was dead, Cory could work on Andrew Vorhees, as next of kin, to use his influence with the DA's office to drop the theft charge. Clearly she had no qualms about using Kenneth — shifting the frame to him had gotten her off the hook so she could plan her revenge — but she cared just enough not to want him to go to prison. As wicked as she was, in her own way she was still her brother's keeper.

Margaret Vorhees' death had been carefully manufactured. And she'd kept herself and Kenneth from being suspects if the police questioned the accident setup by inviting Vorhees to their apartment last night — perfect alibis for both of them. Chaleen was obviously putty in her hands; if he'd had had any qualms about doing the dirty work, she'd beguiled him into it the same way she'd hooked him in the first place — by using sex and the promise of a large cash payoff once she was married to Vorhees. As Tamara said, "Chaleen's the kind of dude who can be bought. Now particularly, with his business in trouble and a string of debts piling up. Plus he's a risk taker, like her. Willing to do whatever's necessary for the big prize."

If Cory suspected it was her brother who was responsible for the tip-off to Runyon, it probably wouldn't matter all that much to her. She'd always been able to control Kenneth, the same as any other man. And she knew that he had no hard evidence to pass along; that without it, Tamara and Jake and I could not afford to take our suspicions to the police. Runyon had done the right thing last night. If I'd been in his place, I'd have kept my mouth shut as well — and hated having to do so as much as he did.

I asked Jake how he thought Kenneth would react to the news of Margaret Vorhees' death.

"If he accuses his sister, she'll just play innocent. The monoxide job looks like an accident — she'll swear to him that it was, that neither she nor Chaleen had anything to do with it."

"But he'll know she's lying. Is there any chance he'll be upset enough to defy her, go to the police on his own?"

"The way I read him, no, not much. More than likely he'll end up doing what he's always done — giving her the benefit of the doubt."

"Real love-hate thing there," Tamara said.

Runyon said, "That's what's tearing him apart. He wants to break loose from her, but he can't do it on his own. Took about all the courage he had to run off to Belardi's, and he only managed that because he's terrified of going to prison."

"Must have some guts to reach out to you the way he has."

"Desperate cry for help, not an act of courage."

I said, "Sees you as an authority figure, a father confessor."

"Pretty much, yeah."

"You think he'll contact you again?"

"He might if he can get away from her long enough to use a phone. Figures she took his cell away from him after bringing him back from Belardi's."

"If you do hear, try to get together with him again in person and convince him to do the right thing. From what you've told us, he's not too coherent on the phone. And you seem to be the only person besides his sister he'll listen to."

Tamara said musingly, "You know, one thing bothers me. That gun Kenny found. He claims Cory never owned a piece before.

And Chaleen didn't use it or need it last night. Then why did she buy it?"

"Protection's the obvious answer."

"Who from? Chaleen? No reason for her to be afraid of lover boy Vorhees."

"That we know about," I said. "She may not have either of them as tightly controlled as we surmise, Chaleen in particular. The gun could be an insurance policy."

"Here's another idea. She bought it for some new scheme she's cooking up."

"Such as?"

"Who knows? Bitch is capable of anything, right? Any damn thing at all."

"Whatever the reason," Runyon said, "I wish I knew what she's done with it. I don't like the idea that it's still in the apartment."

"If it is, she's got it hid this time where Kenny can't find it."

"Let's hope so."

"You don't think she'd use it on him?"

"That's not what worries me."

"Kenny using it on her?"

"Not that, either. I doubt he's capable of harming her, or else he'd have done it long ago."

"Uh, oh. Use it on himself, then?"

"That's it."

I said, "He strike you as potentially suicidal, Jake?"

"No, but there's no way to be sure. He's weak, scared, on the ragged edge. Hates himself as well as his sister. If the trial goes badly, if there's enough pressure to push him over the line, he might decide killing himself is his only way out."

The phone rang just then, as if to add an exclamation point to Jake's words. Tamara slid her chair around to answer the call. Listened, raised an eyebrow in Runyon's direction, listened some more. "I'll see if he's available," she said, tapped the hold button, and said to us, "Andrew Vorhees' secretary. Man wants to see Jake ASAP."

Well, we might have expected it, though not this soon. Runyon and I exchanged glances; he nodded, and I said to Tamara, "Go ahead and make an appointment."

She did that. "Vorhees' office at eleven," she said when she broke the connection. "Man's wife dies last night, he's in his office bright and early this morning. Business as usual."

Runyon said, "He'd say it was his way of keeping his mind off his loss."

"Yeah, sure. What'll you tell him when he asks why you were out at his house?"

"Nothing that'll reflect badly on us. Play it by ear."

"Right."

"There's another way to handle it," I said.

Tamara raised an eyebrow. "What way?"

"Jake and I both keep the appointment. Double up on him. Two are more convincing than one."

"What do you mean, convincing?"

"There doesn't seem to be much we can do to prove Cory and Chaleen are murderers, at least not directly. But there is something we can do to rock the boat she doesn't want rocked. If we work it right, we might even be able to punch enough holes to sink it."

17

When you faced Andrew Vorhees in his plush Civic Center office, it was easy enough to see how he'd been able to forge a successful political and business career despite his scandal-ridden private life. He cut an imposing figure behind a broad cherrywood desk: lean, athletic body encased in a black silk suit that must have cost a couple of thousand dollars, thick dark-curled hair whitening slightly at the temples, craggy features, piercing slate-colored eyes. The kind of self-confident, strong-willed mover-and-shaker who dominates most any room he's in.

If he was bothered at all by the fact that I'd accompanied Runyon, he didn't show it. There was no delay when his secretary announced us, and no visible reaction when she showed us in. Just one question to me: "Who are you?" I told him and he nodded and let the matter drop.

He wore a tight, solemn expression this morning; that and the black suit were his only sops to being newly widowed. If he'd had any feelings left for his dead wife, they were well concealed. When I said, "I'm sorry for your loss, Mr. Vorhees," and Runyon added his condolences in turn, he made a vague gesture as if we'd expressed sorrow over the fact that the weather wasn't better today. He tight-gripped each of our hands for a few seconds while his eyes probed ours: trying to read us and at the same time let us know he was the alpha male here. Jake and I showed him about as much of the inner man as he was showing us, just enough so that he understood we were not intimidated by him.

The first thing he said after we were seated was, "I've never known any private detectives before." He didn't quite make the words "private detectives" sound like an indictment, but close enough.

"A business like any other," I said.

Vorhees picked up a turquoise-and-silver letter opener, held it between thumb and forefinger and tipped it in Runyon's direction. Bluntly, he asked, "Were you working for my wife?"

"No."

"Never had any dealings with her?"

"Not before last night. I never met her while she was alive."

"Then what were you doing at my house?"

"I went there to talk to her."

"About what?"

"Things I felt concerned her."

I said, "The same things I spoke to her about three days ago."

Vorhees frowned at that. "Oh, so *you* had dealings with her."

"Of a sort."

"What does that mean? What did you speak to her about?"

"Relationships, mainly."

"Margaret and I were separated — I suppose you know that."

"I'd heard as much."

"Well?"

"Not your relationship with your wife. Yours with Cory Beckett."

Vorhees' spine stiffened. He made another jabbing motion with the letter opener, toward me this time, before he said, "Even if that were true, my private life is none of your affair. Nor was it any of my wife's affair. I told you, we were legally separated."

"Are you denying a relationship with Cory Beckett?"

"I don't have to confirm or deny anything to you."

"No, you don't. But it so happens I saw you coming out of her apartment building about a week ago. I mentioned it to her, but evidently she didn't mention it to you."

She hadn't. His effort to hide the fact didn't quite come off. "What were you doing there?"

"She was my client at the time. I don't have to tell you she hired our firm to find her brother when he disappeared three weeks ago. One reason I went to see her that day was to inform her that we'd located him, or rather Mr. Runyon had."

"One reason?"

"The other is that I don't like being lied to."

"By Cory Beckett? About what?"

"Why don't you ask her?"

"I'm asking you."

"The theft her brother's charged with," I said. "The fact that it was a frame-up and she was the intended target, not him. The fact that it was her idea he take the blame and that she had help shifting it to him."

The skin across Vorhees' forehead bunched into ribbed rows. He let the letter opener drop with a small clatter on the desktop.

"Bullshit," he said.

"Facts."

"How could you know all that?"

"We're detectives, remember?"

He didn't say anything for a time. Then, "Why would Cory want to frame her brother?"

"Ask her."

"The hell I will. I don't believe it. She loves the kid, she's doing everything she can to get him off. She'd have to be crazy to do what you're accusing her of."

"Or sane and full of schemes."

"Schemes? What kind of schemes?"

"That's not for us to say."

"Why the hell not, if you think you know?"

"Legal and ethical reasons."

"Legal and ethical," he said, as if they were dirty words.

Runyon said, "Aren't you going to ask us who arranged the frame in the first place?"

"If I thought it was true, I wouldn't have to ask."

"Or who allegedly helped her shift it to her brother?"

". . . All right. Who?"

"The same person allegedly recruited to frame her."

"Goddamn it, who?"

"Allegedly," I said, "Frank Chaleen."

The name rocked him like a blow. He got abruptly to his feet, stood woodenly for a clutch of seconds, then leaned forward and flattened his hands on the desktop.

"Bullshit," he said again.

"Fact."

"Cory hardly knows Chaleen."

"She knows him a lot better than you think."

"How do you know she does?"

Runyon said, "When Kenneth ran off, he went to a place called Belardi's on the Petaluma River. That's where I found him. He wouldn't leave with me, so she drove up to convince him and bring him home."

"I know that. So what?"

"Chaleen was with her."

Vorhees started to say something, changed his mind, and opted for a stony silence.

On the ride down here from South Park, Jake and I had decided to push the envelope with him as far as possible. I'd already taken the biggest chance in suggesting, if not directly accusing, Frank Chaleen of complicity in a crime. Now it was time for the capper.

"Chaleen gets around, doesn't he," I said. "One woman at a time's not enough for him. Wives and mistresses, both fair game."

"What the hell does that mean?"

"What do you think it means, if he was involved in the original plan to frame Cory

187

Beckett for theft? It's common knowledge he'd been having an affair with your wife. Seems pretty clear the only thing that would make him switch his allegiance from her to Cory is that he's sleeping with her, too — cuckolding you twice."

A rush of blood put a wine-dark stain on Vorhees' smooth-shaven cheeks. The veins in his neck bulged.

"Sorry," I said, "but it stacks up that way, doesn't it?"

He said between clenched teeth, "That son of a bitch! I'll make him wish he was never born."

Runyon and I let that pass without comment.

The sudden fury didn't last long. Vorhees had not gotten where he was by letting his emotions run away with him. I watched him make a visible effort to control himself.

"You better not be lying to me about any of this," he said at length.

I said, "We're not in the habit of lying."

He lowered himself into his chair, folded his hands together. All business again, except for the fact that the knuckles on both hands showed white. "I've got enough to deal with as it is without the media busting my chops again. What would it take for the two of you to keep all of this quiet?"

"Are you offering us a bribe, Mr. Vorhees?"

"Hell, no. A favor for a favor. I have a fair amount of influence in this city. I could do your agency some good —"

"No, you couldn't. You can't trade for or buy our silence. You already know that if you've checked us out and I'm sure you have. But we'll give it to you for nothing. We didn't intend to make trouble for your wife and we don't intend to make trouble for you. That's not why we've disclosed as much to you as we have."

"No? Then why did you?"

"We don't like to see a good kid like Kenneth Beckett facing a prison sentence for a crime he didn't commit. Or a newly bereaved husband jerked around by lovers and former friends."

"You expect me to believe that?"

"Believe what you like." I got to my feet; Runyon followed suit. "We've said our piece — it's in your hands now."

He made a derisive noise. But his face was set, hard and brittle, like a ceramic sculpture fresh out of the kiln. He believed it, all right. And his simmering anger was not only directed at Chaleen but at his lying, conniving mistress.

Mission accomplished.

Boat rocked and holed and taking on water, fast.

18

JAKE RUNYON

The interview with Andrew Vorhees produced results more quickly than Runyon and Bill had anticipated. That same evening, Kenneth Beckett broke his silence with another call.

"Mrs. Vorhees is dead, Mr. Runyon, you know that," the kid's voice said without preamble. He wasn't calling from home; multiple voices punctuated with laughter rose and fell in the background. "It wasn't an accident. Chaleen did it. I told you, didn't I? You said you wouldn't let it happen."

"I tried, but I got there too late."

"It's my fault. If I'd told you sooner . . ."

"Ken, listen to me. Where are you now?"

"A tavern down the block. Mr. Vorhees came to the apartment again tonight. He was mad, real mad — he knows about Cory fucking Chaleen. He kept yelling at her, calling her names, and she kept yelling back. They forgot about me so I sneaked out and came here."

"What's the name of the tavern?"

". . . I don't know."

"Ask somebody. I'll come there and we'll talk. Decide what to do."

"Can't we just talk now? I don't want to be away too long. They might . . . Cory might come looking for me."

"I can barely hear you with all the background noise. Better if we talk in person anyway. Find out the name of the tavern, okay?"

There was a short silence. Then the bar sounds cut off — Beckett must have put his hand over the mouthpiece. After the better part of a minute, "It's the Fox and Hounds. On Pine Street."

"It shouldn't take me more than half an hour to get there. Promise me you'll wait."

"All right. As long as Cory doesn't come."

The Ford's GPS got Runyon to Pine Street and into a legal parking space in twenty-seven minutes. The Fox and Hounds was an upscale Nob Hill version of a British pub: horseshoe-shaped bar, dark wood booths, dartboards, framed fox-hunting prints, signs advertising a dozen varieties of British ales and lagers. There were maybe twenty patrons, most of them in the booths and grouped in front of one of a pair of dartboards where a noisy match was going on. Beckett wasn't among them.

So the kid hadn't waited after all. Faded in, made his call, lost his nerve and faded out. Like a shadow —

No, he *was* still here. Must've been in the men's room because he emerged from a hallway at the rear, moving in a slow, slump-shouldered walk, and went to sit in front of a full glass of beer at the far end of the bar. He was staring into the glass when Runyon got to him.

"Ken."

Beckett's head jerked up. Fear showed in his face, visible even in the dim lighting, until he recognized Runyon; then it morphed into a kind of twitchy relief. "I thought you'd never get here," he said. "I almost left a couple of times."

"I'm glad you didn't. Let's go sit in a booth. More privacy."

There was one empty booth, just vacated and at a distance from the dart throwers; Runyon claimed it for them. A waitress appeared, began clearing the table, and asked them what they'd like. Beckett shook his head; he'd left his beer on the bar, probably hadn't drunk much, if any, of it. Runyon ordered a pint of Bass ale, but only because it was necessary to remain in the booth.

When the waitress went away, he said to Beckett, "Now we can talk. About Mrs. Vorhees' death, first. What did Cory say about it?"

"She said it was an accident, a fortunate accident. Fortunate for me because now for sure I wouldn't have to go to prison." The kid was facing toward the entrance; he cast a nervous look in that direction before he went on. "But I could tell she was lying. I can always tell."

"You didn't say anything to her about your suspicions?"

"They're not suspicions. She made Chaleen kill Mrs. Vorhees."

"Made him?"

"I told you before, she can make anybody do anything she wants. Any man."

Beckett was looking toward the entrance again. Runyon touched his arm to refocus his attention. "You want to be free of her, don't you, Ken? Free to live your own life, work on yachts like the *Ocean Queen* again."

"Yeah, sure, but it's too late now."

"No, it isn't. Not if you tell the police everything you've told me."

"The police? No! I couldn't do that.

They'd think I was guilty, too, like they think I stole Mrs. Vorhees' necklace."

"Not if I go with you, vouch for you."

Violent headshake. Badly agitated now, couldn't seem to keep his hands still; they moved on the table, folding, clenching, unfolding, scrabbling away from each other with the fingers hooked upward like a pair of white spiders. "I won't go to the police. I *can't*. If you try to force me . . ."

"I wouldn't do that. I'm only thinking of what's best for you. I haven't betrayed your trust in me so far, have I?"

". . . No."

"Okay. You're positive Cory and Chaleen conspired to murder Mrs. Vorhees. You don't want them to get away with it, do you?"

"No."

"Then you have to do something. What do you think it should be?"

Headshake. "I don't know. I don't know *what* to do. Just not the police. . . ."

"Then we'll figure out another way together." Runyon let a few seconds pass before he asked, "Does Cory have any idea that you suspect her and Chaleen?"

"I don't think so. I didn't say anything to make her suspicious."

"What would she have done if you had?"

"Done?"

"She wouldn't hurt you, would she?"

"No. Not like . . . no."

"Has she ever hurt you, Ken?"

"Slaps a few times, that's all." He winced as he said the words, as if he could still feel the sting of those slaps. "She wouldn't do anything if she knew that I know, just lie and tell me I'm being silly. She keeps saying after the trial everything will be like it used to be, but that's a lie, too. It's only going to get worse."

"Why do you say that?"

"Mrs. Vorhees . . . that wasn't the end of it."

"You think she's planning something else?"

The waitress reappeared with the pint of Bass, waited for Runyon to pay and tip her before she moved off. Beckett was again staring toward the entrance, his hands still crawling the table. Runyon had the feeling that if his sister were to come in, the kid would immediately slide down and try to hide under the table.

He said, "Ken. *Do* you think Cory's planning something else, some other crime?"

Six-beat, while a shout went up from the dart players. Then, when the noise died down, "Something, yeah. I just hope . . ."

"What do you hope?"

Headshake.

"Do you have any idea what it might be?"

"No. I wish to God I did."

"Is there any way you can find out?"

"How? She won't tell me anything, just lies and more lies. And she's careful now when she talks on the phone to Chaleen."

"Does he come to the apartment to see her?"

"No. She goes out to crawl in bed with him."

"He's never been there?"

"Never. Only Mr. Vorhees —"

Somebody must have come into the tavern just then; Beckett stiffened with his head craned forward like a pointer. But the new arrival wasn't his sister or anybody else he knew. He sagged back again, drew a shaky breath before his pale eyes met Runyon's again.

Runyon said, "Do you know what Cory did with the gun you told me about?"

"Gun? Oh, Jesus, the gun. . . ."

"Is it still in the apartment?"

"I don't know. Maybe she put it in her car. Or gave it to Chaleen."

"Why would she give it to him?"

"I don't know, I don't know why she does anything."

"Have you looked for it?"

Headshake. "I can't while she's there. And she locks me in my room now when she goes out and when she's in bed with Mr. Vorhees. I tried picking the lock, but I couldn't do it. . . ."

Good enough, Runyon thought. One worry eased. You couldn't use a weapon on yourself if you had no idea where it was and no opportunity to hunt for it.

Beckett's gaze shifted away from him again. "I can't stay any longer, Mr. Runyon, I have to get back. Mr. Vorhees is probably gone by now and she'll be looking for me and she'll be mad."

"All right. But before you go, tell me what Mr. Vorhees said to Cory when he showed up tonight."

"Oh, he was pissed, really pissed, about her letting Chaleen do it to her. He called her all kinds of names. Slut, bitch, whore."

"Did he say how he found out?"

"I don't remember if he did."

"Did she deny the affair with Chaleen?"

"Yeah, but he didn't believe her. He told her he'd make her pay for two-timing him with that bastard. Make both of them pay."

"Make them pay how?"

Headshake. "That's when I couldn't stand it anymore, when I snuck out."

"Did he seem to have any idea Cory and Chaleen were responsible for his wife's death?"

"He didn't say anything about that." Beckett flattened his hands on the table, shoved himself upright — movements so frantic they nearly upset the glass of ale. "I have to go now. Please."

"Okay. Just remember, I'm available whenever you want to talk again. Any time, day or night."

"Thanks, I —" The kid broke off as if struck by a sudden thought, blinked a couple of times, and then said, "Jesus, the trial. It's coming soon, on Monday. Will you be there, Mr. Runyon? It won't be so bad for me if you are."

"Count on it."

Beckett nodded once, shaped his mouth into what was probably meant to be a smile but came off more like a grimace, then rushed for the door and was gone into the night.

The Becketts were already in the Civic Center courtroom, seated at the defendant's table with their lawyer, Sam Wasserman, when Runyon walked in Monday morning. Both of them dressed in dark conservative clothing, Kenneth uncomfortable-looking in a suit and tie, his sister calm and cool behind a mask of solemn concern. She sat close to him, shoulders touching, her hand on his clenched fingers on the table.

Not many of the seats in the spectator section were occupied. Andrew Vorhees was not among the handful of people seated there; neither was Frank Chaleen. The only person Runyon recognized was a *Chronicle* reporter, probably looking for an angle he could use to stir up fresh interest in a socialite's "accidental" death. A couple of the others would also be newshounds, the rest the type of courthouse junkies who attend felony trials at random for their own amusement.

He sat down in the front row to the far right of the defendant's table, where both of the Becketts would be sure to see him. The kid spotted him first; some of the rigidity in his posture seemed to ease and an expression that might have been gratitude or relief animated his thin face. Cory followed his gaze, frowned briefly when she saw Runyon, then whispered something to her brother that made him turn his head to face the bench and keep it there. After that one glance at Runyon, she ignored him. Making it obvious that to her his presence was nothing more than a minor annoyance: he had nothing to do with the matter at hand.

Vorhees still hadn't put in an appearance when the judge, a stern-faced woman in her fifties, came out of chambers and the bailiff called the proceedings to order.

Runyon had expected the trial to last a minimum of one full day, but it was over in less than half an hour — aborted by a nolle prosequi from an Assistant DA. The reason given was that the complainant was recently deceased and her next of kin — her husband — didn't wish to pursue prosecution; therefore the DA's office had decided to accede to his wishes and was recommending that the charges against the defendant be dropped. The Becketts' high-priced lawyer didn't have to say a word in his client's defense. The judge delivered a brief lecture to Kenneth warning against the dire consequences of any repeat offense, and banged her gavel.

Case dismissed.

Cory embraced her brother, whispered something to him that caused his head to bob up and down. He looked a little stunned, as if he couldn't quite wrap his mind around the verdict. Runyon thought he might be able to edge in for a word with Beckett, but she didn't let that happen. She hustled the kid out of the courtroom without a glance in Runyon's direction, the bulky Wasserman helping her run interference. The reporters followed them out, yammering for interviews, but their luck wasn't any better.

Runyon was the last to leave. On his way out of the building he was thinking that the fallout from the talk with Andrew Vorhees had been just what he and Bill hoped for. They'd not only managed to destroy or drive a deep wedge into Vorhees' relationship with Cory Beckett, but to convince him to let her brother off the hook. There was always the chance that he'd be angry and vindictive enough to pay her back in part by hurting her brother, but given what they knew about him and his methods, and what they'd told him about the frame-up, the odds were good that he'd do just what he had done — declined to pursue prosecution.

Besides, they'd had some insurance: even if Vorhees had pressed the theft charge, Sam Wasserman would likely have gotten Beckett off. The DA's case was shaky with the plaintiff dead and no one else to testify directly on her behalf, and losing it would have been a black mark on an already less-than stellar record in this election year. The DA would have been only too willing to let the whole thing drop.

So far so good. Question now was, how would the Vorhees/Cory Beckett/Chaleen mess play out? Volatile, secretive, parlous bunch, capable of just about any action or reaction, which made anticipating what any of them would do next difficult, if not impossible. Runyon's one hope was that whatever happened, poor Kenneth Beckett wouldn't get caught in the middle again.

19

"I want to establish a memorial for Cybil," Kerry said. "So she won't be forgotten."

She announced this as we were finishing dinner that night, without having said anything along those lines previously. She'd been quiet up until then, the thoughtful kind of quiet. Cybil's death had left her subdued but not withdrawn; she seemed to be coping with it well enough, her grief neither entirely locked up inside nor morbid in her outward expressions of it. She hadn't thrown herself compulsively into her work at Bates and Carpenter or in her office here in the condo, or avoided normal contact with Emily and me, or suffered onsets of depression in which she suddenly burst into tears. And her appetite had been reasonably good. But it was obvious that Cybil remained uppermost in her thoughts and that she'd had this memorial idea, whatever it was, for some time and was only now ready to share it.

Emily and I exchanged glances; her expressive eyes told me she had no more idea than I did what Kerry meant. Wasn't that corner of her office she'd devoted to Cybil's possessions a kind of memorial?

I said, "We're not about to forget her, babe, you know that."

"Not ever," Emily said. "We'll always remember her and love her."

"I know that," Kerry said. "We won't forget her, but what about the rest of the world? If we don't do something to preserve her memory, it'll be as if she never existed."

I pushed my plate away and reached over to touch her hand. "That's not true. There are those two novels of hers —"

"Both out of print now."

"— and plenty of readers and collectors like me who remember her stories for the pulps."

"Yes, exactly. But not enough of them. How many pulp collectors have actually read Cybil's stories? Not many, I'll bet. Most collectors are only interested in owning the magazines for their investment value, or their artwork, or because they contain stories by famous writers — you told me that yourself. And what few pulps come up for sale on eBay and elsewhere these days are expensive, prohibitively so for all but individuals with deep pockets. That's true, too, isn't it?"

I admitted that it was.

She said, "But there is enough interest in pulp fiction among modern readers to make collections and anthologies of obscure pulp stories profitable for small-press publishers. There are several that specialize in that type of book — you've bought a few of those reprints yourself."

I knew what she was getting at now. "You want to try to sell a collection of Cybil's Max Ruffe stories. That's what you meant by memorial."

"Yes. I've been rereading some of them and they're really very good — and I'm not saying that because she was my mother. Cybil was a fine stylist, a clever plotter."

And had a real knack, I thought, for writing the kind of tough-guy fiction her male counterparts were turning out then and now. The only woman of her generation I could think of who did it as well was Leigh Brackett. It had always been puzzling to me why Cybil's work had slipped into relative obscurity, while male writers from the forties and fifties of lesser talent had gained various measures of popularity.

Kerry was saying, "But I don't mean just

a single collection of her stories. There are twenty-seven in all, most of them novelettes, and one in *Midnight Detective* that's a short novel. There'd have to be at least three volumes to include them all. That's doable, isn't it?"

"I don't see why not."

"And reprints of *Dead Eye* and *Black Eye*, too. The complete Max Ruffe, by Cybil Wade writing as Samuel Leatherman." She was more animated now, a little crackle of excitement in her voice. "Also doable?"

"Probably. But the original publisher of the two novels is out of business now and I doubt a major house would be interested. It'd have to be a small press, probably a print-on-demand outfit."

"One that does e-books, too," Emily said.

"Right. There are several out there."

"And Mom could write the introductions."

Kerry said, "That's just what I was thinking. And not only commentary on the stories, but on Cybil's life — a series of personal memoirs. I could do it, I think — do justice to her and her work."

"I'll bet it'd be easier than writing advertising copy," Emily said.

Kerry shifted her gaze to me, her eyes as bright as I'd seen them in a long time.

"What do you think? Can we convince one of those small publishers to reprint all of Cybil's fiction?"

"We can sure give it a try."

"Good! You know which ones are most likely to be receptive. I'll write the pitch letters if you'll give me their names."

"Better yet," I said, "we'll pick them out together."

So after we finished supper, Kerry and I went into her office and used her computer to pull up the websites of publishers specializing in mystery and detective pulp fiction reprints in both print-on-demand and e-book editions, paying particular attention to their production values and cover art. There were two I'd recommended that Kerry liked as well, and two more we picked out together. At least one of the four ought to be interested; if not, there were a few others we could try.

"I wish we'd done this when Cybil was alive," she said. "I mentioned the idea to her once, but she wasn't interested. She never had a high regard for her fiction." Kerry added wryly, "Unlike Ivan, who thought his work was about half a rung below the level of genius. Or pretended to."

"Hers was better."

"By a wide margin. I'm really glad you

think this is a good idea."

"A very good idea," I said, and meant it.

She said she wanted to get started right away on drafting a proposal, so I left her to it and went back into the living room. And there was Emily, curled up on the couch reading one of Cybil's Max Ruffe stories in a 1947 issue of *Midnight Detective* on which Samuel Leatherman had been cover-featured. Modern kid, fourteen years old and raised on computers, engrossed in the mouldering pages of a type of popular culture that had flourished more than half a century before she was born.

I sat down quietly so as not to disturb her, thinking that where women were concerned, I was a pretty lucky guy. All the women in my life, dating back to my childhood, had been special. My mother, and Nana, her mother. Kerry. Emily. Cybil. Tamara. All but one of the half dozen or so I'd been involved with before I met Kerry, even though those relationships, for one reason or another, hadn't lasted. Smart, caring, loving, every one.

Thank God for women like them. And that there were only a few, a very few, of the ones like Cory Beckett.

Tuesday was not one of my scheduled days

at the office. But after I finished a couple of errands I didn't feel much like rattling around at home, so I gave in to impulse and drove down to South Park. I didn't expect any new developments on the Vorhees/Cory Beckett matter since yesterday's trial dismissal of the theft charge against Kenneth Beckett, but Tamara had one waiting for me when I walked in.

"I was just about to call you," she said. "You'd think Andrew Vorhees would be pissed at us, right? Well, he's not. He called for another appointment not fifteen minutes ago — the big man himself this time, not one of his flunkies. Seems he wants to engage our services, as he put it."

"Oh? To do what?"

"Hedged on that, said he'd discuss it in person. Could be something to do with his wife's death, but I'll bet he's after as much dirt as we can dig up on Cory. Chaleen, too."

"Payback ammunition."

"Yep."

"What did you tell him?"

"I didn't commit us, just said we'd listen to what he has to say. But if it's Cory and Chaleen he's after, why not take him on? His money's good and the dirt is already about nine-tenths dug up."

"Did he ask for me, Jake, or both of us?"

"You. But I told him he'd probably get Jake instead and he said okay."

"Why Jake instead?"

"Well, he wants to have the meeting tonight — eight o'clock, on his yacht. Said he'll be tied up with other matters all day and something to take care of after he leaves his office. Probably true — he didn't stay on the line long and he sounded hassled. I figured you'd rather spend the evening with Kerry and Emily. And Jake's up for it — I just got off the phone with him."

"Fine by me. He'll get as much if not more out of Vorhees as I would."

"We'll know a lot more about what's happening with Cory and Chaleen when he reports in," Tamara said. Her smile was wolfish. "And with any luck, a legitimate reason to stay involved in this mess and a fat cat's fat check for all our troubles."

At two-thirty I was still at my desk, fiddling with a report on a routine skip-trace. I had written scores like it before, but today, for some reason, I was having trouble getting the gist of it down in coherent English. Committing words to paper, or now to a computer screen, is not one of my long suits; I have to drag them together into intelligible sentences at the best of times. It was a good thing Kerry intended to write all the introductory material for Cybil's collected works; I'd have been worthless as a collaborator. I was staring off into space, trying to think of a way to frame what should have been a simple statement of fact, when the outer door to the anteroom opened.

Except that it didn't just open; it thumped and rattled as if it had been pushed in hard. Sharp clicking steps followed. I couldn't see who had come in because my office door was partly closed. Alex Chavez was in the anteroom, working on his laptop at one of the desks, and I heard the mutter of his voice and then a kind of cat-hiss response. Even before Alex came and poked his head in and said I had a visitor, I knew who it was.

She was standing alone in the middle of the anteroom, straight as a tree with her arms down at her sides and her mouth so tightly compressed it seemed lipless. Dressed in an expensive scarlet outfit today — suit, shoes, scarf, purse — that made her midnight hair seem even blacker, the red color scheme broken only by a white cashmere turtleneck and a gold cameo brooch. This was the other Cory Beckett, the real Cory Beckett. Nothing soft or seductive about her. Hard. Glacial. All the fire burned deep inside — a molten core wrapped in a block of ice.

Chavez stood looking at her from a distance with his mouth open a little, as if he'd never seen anyone quite like her before. Tamara was there, too, standing in the doorway to her office; she glanced at me as I stepped out, but only for a second. Cory Beckett had her full attention. She didn't have to have met the woman before to know who she was.

Cory's magnetic gaze was fixed on me, unblinking, as I approached her. Sub-zero cubes of luminous gray-green glittering with venom. Touch her skin, I thought, and you'd burn your fingers. Like touching dry ice.

I said, "Well, Ms. Beckett, this is a surprise," even though it wasn't. After nearly forty years in law enforcement, hardly anything surprises me anymore.

"Is it?" Her voice had a brittle quality, as if it, too, were partially frozen. "I don't think so, after what you and what's-his-name that works for you did."

"What did we do?"

"Don't play games with me. Your lies to Andrew Vorhees almost cost my brother his freedom."

"We didn't tell him any lies. Just repeated yours."

"I ought to sue you for slander."

"But you won't because you know you have no case. We never accused you of anything, or even once took your name in vain. Ask Vorhees, if you haven't already."

Her mouth worked and puckered as if she were about to spit. Instead she said, "Damn you, you might've helped send Kenny to prison."

"But that didn't happen. You were confident he'd get off, and that's exactly what did happen. He didn't even have to stand trial."

"No thanks to you."

I smiled at her. "How's your relationship going with Vorhees, by the way? Wedding bells in the offing? After a decent period of mourning, of course."

No reaction. Cory ice.

"More likely he's getting ready to bounce you out of his life, if he hasn't already. That's the real reason you're here, isn't it?"

"Fuck you."

"Such language. Did you know he's thinking of hiring us?"

She hadn't known. It was three blinks before she said, "Hire you? To do what?"

"He hasn't said yet. Maybe to investigate you."

"What? He wouldn't do that."

"Sure he would," I said. "You and Frank Chaleen. Not very smart of you to try juggling two affairs at the same time with prominent men who don't get along."

The icebound venom in her eyes was so intense now it darkened the irises, made them seem like black holes. She said, spitting the words, "My personal life is none of your business."

"It is if this agency is paid to conduct a legal investigation and what we find out is a matter of public record."

"I won't stand for being harassed."

"No one is harassing you. Except possibly Andrew Vorhees."

"I'm warning you," she said. "Leave me and my brother alone. If you make any trouble for us, bother us in any way ever again, you'll regret it."

"Threats in front of witnesses, Ms. Beckett?"

She stood shredding me with those eyes, a stare-down that went on for maybe fifteen seconds. Then she did the one thing I was not expecting — the thing, I realized afterward, she'd come here intending to do.

Without warning, cat-quick, she stepped

forward and belted me open-handed across the face.

It was a hell of a blow. She was no lightweight; there was considerable strength in that slender body. I staggered backward a step from the force of it, bells going off in my head, before I recovered my equilibrium. She stayed put long enough to watch with chilly satisfaction as I lifted my hand, grimacing, and then she spun on her heel and stalked out.

Chavez, still gawking, murmured something in Spanish. Even Tamara was impressed. She said from her office doorway, "Wow, that was some slap. You okay?"

My cheek stung like fury. Touching it with fingertips made me wince. "I'll live."

"You're lucky the bitch didn't use her nails."

"Yeah," I said. "Or her gun."

20

JAKE RUNYON

It was full dark when Runyon pulled into the parking lot next to the St. Francis Yacht Club. This part of the city was ablaze with lights after nightfall — rectangles, blobs, streamers, shimmers from the Marina District homes, the Palace of Fine Arts, the rushing traffic on Marina Boulevard, and closer in here, stationary lights at the club building, along the West Harbor walkways and floats, on a few of the boats anchored in the basin. The combined light-glare made the water and the overcast sky look like sections of sunstruck black glass.

There weren't many cars in the lot, and no one in sight as he followed the walkway to the gate nearest the slip where Andrew Vorhees' yacht was berthed. He expected the *Ocean Queen* to be one of the lighted craft, but it was just a bulky shadow-shape in its slip, showing no illumination of any kind.

Runyon checked the radium dial on his Timex: 7:56. Vorhees should be here waiting for him by now. And should have left the security gate open or unlocked for access to the yacht. It was neither.

Delayed for some reason. Busy man, Vorhees, the demands on his time increased now by the load of personal problems weighing on him. Even relatively important appointments, as this one would seem to be, were subject to obstruction of one kind or another.

A need for movement set him pacing the walkway from one end to the other. Still no sign of Vorhees after half a dozen or more back-and-forth treks. He went back to the parking lot. Tamara had given him Vorhees' cell number, but his call went straight to voice mail. He left a terse message, giving the time and his location; Vorhees already had his number, in the exchange with Tamara, but he added it anyway.

He swung the Ford around and reparked it so that it was facing Yacht Road. The agency file included the fact that Vorhees drove a two-year-old silver Aston Martin. Should be easy to spot when he finally showed up.

Except that he didn't show up.

Eight-thirty, nine — no sign of him.

And no return call.

Runyon tapped the redial button on his cell. As before, the call went straight to Vorhees' voice mail. No point in leaving a second message. He quit the car, walked back along the concrete strip to where the dark shape of the *Ocean Queen* loomed below.

The restlessness in him intensified. This lengthy a delay didn't seem right. Vorhees was a public-sector, politically connected businessman, the kind of man who didn't blow off meetings on a whim; if he was going to be this late for an appointment that he'd initiated, he should have made contact and given a reason by now.

Brisk footsteps sounded on the walkway behind Runyon. But it wasn't Vorhees. A pudgy, sixtyish man in a yachting cap approached the gate, stopped, and gave him a curious but not unfriendly glance. "Hi there," he said. "Don't know you, do I?"

"Afraid not. I'm here to see Andrew Vorhees. Business matter."

"Oh, sure. Poor Andy. You know his wife died in an accident a few days ago?"

"Yes."

"Terrible thing. Terrible." The pudgy

yachtsman shook his head, then peered in the direction of Vorhees' yacht. "Doesn't look like he's aboard."

Runyon said, "Belowdecks, maybe." He didn't really believe it.

Neither did the yachtsman. "Could be," he said dubiously, "but he'd have to be sitting in the dark. You'd see a light otherwise."

"All right if I go aboard and check? Wait for him on deck if he's not here yet?"

"Well . . . You're here on business, you say?"

"That's right."

"Kind of late in the day, isn't it?"

"Mr. Vorhees has been tied up all day. This is the only time he had free." Runyon added his name and the agency's name, omitting the fact that they were a firm of private investigators.

The pudgy man subjected him to a closer scrutiny, decided he was who he said he was and that there was no need to ask for his ID. "I guess it'll be okay," he said. "My name's Greenwood. I own the *Belle Epoch,* two slips down from Andy's."

"Nice to meet you, Mr. Greenwood."

Greenwood opened the gate with a key and they went together down the ramp to the board float that stretched between the slips. At the *Ocean Queen,* Runyon thanked the man and swung himself on board. Greenwood stood for a moment watching as Runyon went to the main cabin door and rapped on it, then moved on when there was no response from within.

When the yachtsman had passed out of sight, Runyon tried the door. Secure. The afterdeck benches were covered by tarps to weather-protect the cushions; he sat on the one on the port side where he could watch the walkway and gate above.

More time passed. Quiet here, peaceful, though it didn't do much to cure his unease. Muted traffic noises from out on the boulevard, classical music playing softly on one of the other boats. A breeze had picked up and the night temperature had dropped several degrees, but he barely noticed. Weather conditions meant little to him unless they had a direct effect on a job he was doing. When it got hot enough or cold enough, his bad leg — the one busted in half a dozen places in the highspeed car crash that had killed his partner and effectively ended his Seattle police career — ached and stiffened and sometimes hampered his movements.

Being on a luxury yacht like this one had no meaning for him, either. Boating wasn't his thing; his experience with watercraft of any kind was limited. Skiffs and rowboats the few times he'd tried fishing, a sport he'd eventually decided wasn't for him. The only time he'd enjoyed being on a boat was when he and Colleen had gone sailing on Puget Sound with casual friends who owned a small sloop. When was that? Three . . . no, four years after they were married. That had been a pretty good day. Bright sun, calm water, just enough wind to billow the sails and keep the sloop moving. But the main reason he'd enjoyed it was because Colleen had.

Thinking about that long-ago day brought up an image of her standing next to the main mast. Head tilted skyward, gamin face in perfect profile, long fair hair feathered and swirled by the wind. Tall and slender in blue shorts and white halter, the sun radiant on her long legs and bare midriff. She'd always been beautiful to him, but that day, watching her framed against sun and sky and blue water, she'd taken his breath away. And made him wonder yet again why she'd picked him to fall in love with out of all the men she could've had, a dedicated cop who laid his life on the line every day, a divorced man paying child support to an unbalanced alcoholic ex-wife who'd taken his son away from him, a flawed man who didn't share half her passions, preferred staying at home to traveling, had to be talked into social outings like this one. He'd asked her that question once, in all seriousness, and she'd just smiled and said that a good man was far more important to her than a perfect one and besides, you love who you love and it doesn't really matter why.

Funny. Since her death he had taken out and savored many memories of their time together, like you would favorite photographs in a family album. But that day on the sloop, the image of her standing there in the wind and sun, hadn't been one of them. Why not?

Then he remembered why not.

As he'd watched her, a rush of emotion had welled up and on impulse he'd gone to her and taken her in his arms and kissed her with no little passion — surprising himself because he was not a man given to spontaneous displays of affection in the presence of others. "Well, what prompted that?" she'd said, pleased, maintaining the embrace, and he'd said, "Thinking what a lucky guy I am to be married to you." And she'd smiled and said, "I feel the same about you. Colleen and Jake, two of the luckiest people in the world."

Lucky. Two of the luckiest people in the world.

Until all the luck suddenly ran out. . . .

The creak of footfalls on the float alerted him, shoved the memory back into storage. But the approaching steps didn't belong to Vorhees. The tread came from the other direction — the pudgy yachtsman, Greenwood, returning. He paused alongside the *Ocean Queen,* peering upward at where Runyon was seated.

"Still no sign of Andy yet, eh?" he said.

"Not yet."

"You try calling him?"

"Twice."

"Held up on account of what happened to his wife, maybe. He's a pretty important man and something terrible like that happens, well, it sets off a media bombshell. Those people can be relentless."

Runyon agreed that they could.

"Or could be political or union business. That what you're here to see him about?"

"No. Private matter."

"Oh, I see," Greenwood said, the way people do when they really don't see at all. "You planning to wait much longer? Getting pretty cold out."

"A while. It's important that I see him."

"Well, in that case, my wife thought you

might like something to drink to keep you warm. Coffee, tea, a hot toddy."

"Good of you both, thanks, but I'll pass," Runyon said. "Mind if I ask you a question, Mr. Greenwood?"

"Fire away."

"Have you seen Mr. Vorhees anywhere this evening? Say since four or five o'clock?"

Greenwood didn't have to think about it. "No," he said, "and I would have if he'd been at the club or around the harbor. I was here all day. Haven't seen him since last night."

"What time was that?"

"Oh, about this time. Maybe a little later."

"Was he alone or with someone?"

"Alone. Seemed to be pretty upset — his wife, I imagine. He didn't even want to hear condolences."

Runyon thanked him again, gave an appropriate response when Greenwood asked him to make sure the security gate was locked after him whenever he left, and another when the yachtsman said good night. Alone again, he sat with his mind a blank slate, the door to his memories locked tight.

The half hour between nine-thirty and ten came and went. By then he was aware of the cold because his bad leg had begun to give out little twinges. At a few minutes past ten he called it quits, more than just restlessness working in him.

A high-powered, determined type like Vorhees being late for an appointment was one thing. Failing to show for it without calling or returning calls was something else again.

Runyon drove from the yacht harbor to Nob Hill. There was no reason to suppose that Vorhees had decided to pay another visit to Cory Beckett, but he had to be somewhere and she was capable of appeasing his anger and luring him back into her bed. Sex was as good a reason as any for a man, even one as tough-minded as Vorhees, failing to keep a business appointment.

The facing windows of the Becketts' apartment were all dark, but it was getting on toward eleven o'clock; Cory could just as well be in bed alone. Runyon didn't see the Aston Martin in the immediate vicinity, but Vorhees was too intelligent to park a six-figure set of wheels on a public street, even in an upper-class neighborhood like this. The nearest open-all-night garage was in the next block west; Runyon pulled in there, described the silver sports job to the sleepy-eyed attendant.

"Oh, sure, I know that car. Some sweet ride. Belongs to a VIP — Andrew Vorhees."

"That's right. He been in tonight?"

"Not since I came on at six. Left the Aston here a couple of hours last night, but not tonight."

The Vorhees house in St. Francis Wood was dark except for the night-light on the porch. The driveway was empty, the yellow DO NOT CROSS police strip still in place across the front of the garage. No cars on the street in the vicinity, either.

Runyon made two more phone calls on his way down Sloat Boulevard. Knowing they wouldn't buy him anything, doing it anyway because he was always thorough. The first, to Vorhees' cell, again went to voice mail. The second, to his home number, went unanswered.

Whereabouts unaccounted for and incommunicado all evening. Maybe there was a simple explanation, maybe there wasn't, but whatever the reason Runyon didn't like the feel of it. Not one bit.

21

FRANK CHALEEN

He sat alone in his office, guzzling single-malt scotch and worrying, worrying. About Cory, Vorhees, Chaleen Manufacturing. About himself and his future. The wall clock read 6:30. Everybody gone for the day but him, and the only reason he was still here was because he had nowhere else to go. He'd be just as alone, just as worried in his Cow Hollow flat.

Spread out on the desk in front of him were the P&L printouts Abby had left for him. He kept trying to tell himself they were full of discrepancies, misconceptions, but he knew they weren't; Abby was too good a bookkeeper to make mistakes. The statements might as well have been printed in red ink. Drowning in it the past six months — the miserable goddamn economy. Orders and profits way down, creditors yammering for payment of overdue bills, accounts receivable not much more than two-thirds of the operating expenses and getting harder and harder to collect.

Projections for the next six months didn't look much better. He'd had to lay off three workers this past year, might have to let another go pretty soon. Couldn't afford to replace the extrusion machine that kept breaking down, and if it crapped out completely, they'd have trouble filling the orders that did come in. At the rate things were going, and without an infusion of cash, he might be able to keep Chaleen Manufacturing afloat another a year or so before his creditors and the fucking bank forced him into Chapter Eleven.

Maybe he should have listened to the old man's advice. Don't be too ambitious, don't try to expand too soon, don't overextend the profit margin. But Christ, the old man had always been dispensing advice like that, trying to mold him in his own tight-fisted, tight-assed image. Don't throw your money around, Frank, don't chase women, don't gamble, don't do this, don't do that. And what had his conservative business practices and vanilla lifestyle gotten him? A heart attack and a hole in the ground at fifty-two without ever really having lived. That wasn't Frank Chaleen's way. Never had been, never would be.

Still, there was no denying the bind he was in now. Banks wouldn't give him a new loan, not for any amount, not with all that red ink; he'd already been turned down half a dozen times. Nobody would float him a private loan, either, none of the rich bastards he'd met in his City Hall days — Vorhees had seen to that. Even Margaret had turned him down, and all he'd asked her for was fifty thousand. "You know I don't believe in loaning money to anyone for any reason, Frank. And I won't make an exception for you. You're a wonderful lover but a poor businessman." Bitch. She'd deserved what she got the other night —

No. He didn't want to think any more about Margaret.

He shuffled the P&L statements together, banged the rose quartz paperweight down on the pile. Fifty thousand wouldn't save the company, but it would've helped hold the wolves at bay a while longer — bought the new extrusion machine so the present production pace could be maintained, kept the bills more or less current until the economy finally started turning around. Fifty thousand. Cory'd promised she could get him that much out of Vorhees once she was married to the bugger, and there'd be a whole lot more when they figured a safe way to get rid of Vorhees and she inherited. She'd keep her promises, too; he wouldn't have let her talk him into doing the things he'd done for her if he didn't believe that.

Except that now all of a sudden everything was up in the air. That frigging Runyon and his boss. How the hell had they found out Cory was sleeping with him, too? That fit Vorhees had thrown at her last night, after those two put the bug in his ear . . . she said it could've been worse but it was bad enough. She'd played innocent, calmed him down, let him screw her again, but Vorhees wouldn't be that easily satisfied. No telling what he might do, especially if he got a whiff that Margaret's death wasn't an accident. He could be a pit bull when he was crossed. Chaleen had learned that when he'd mistakenly decided to have a fling at city politics and worked on the bastard's campaign for supervisor. Did those two private snoops suspect the truth about Margaret, put that bug in Vorhees' ear, too? Runyon was the one who'd found her body. . . .

Cory said no, Vorhees didn't doubt the official verdict of a drunken accident. Said Vorhees wasn't going to walk out on her, either, she wouldn't let that happen. Stay cool, Frank, be patient; nothing's changed, it's still going to go according to plan. Well, what else could he do? In too deep now not to trust she knew what she was doing, but it didn't keep him from worrying.

The worst of it was her insisting they stop seeing each other until she was sure Vorhees was no longer suspicious and would own up to his marriage proposal. Even an hour or two together somewhere out of town was too risky. So he was looking at days, weeks, without her. Along with everything else weighing heavy on him, he wasn't sure he could stand that.

Just remember I love you, Frank. As if he could forget it. Christ! He loved her just as much if not more. Never imagined he could feel about any woman the way he felt about Cory. But then he'd never imagined a woman remotely like her existed anywhere on the planet. Smart. Ruthless. A little wild, a little scary. Unique. Exciting. Best sex he'd ever had, ever hoped to have. Incredible sex.

Took his breath away the first time he saw her naked. . . .

Don't think about that, either. All he was doing was giving himself a useless hard-on.

He drained the last of the scotch, got up to pour a refill at the wet bar. Back at his desk, he stared at the pile of P&L statements without touching them again. A sudden sharp surge of frustration made him slam his fist down on the blotter hard enough to rattle the objects on the desktop. He caught up his glass before it spilled, took another pull.

Somewhere out front, the sound of a car engine broke the silence. Growing louder, coming onto company property; Abby must have forgotten to lock the gates when she left. But it wouldn't be her coming back, not this late. Who the hell — ?

A squeal of tires as the driver braked near the office building. The slam of a car door. And a few seconds later, he heard the outer door open and then bang shut.

He knew who it was by then and he was on his feet when Andrew Vorhees came through into his private office. In spite of himself he felt a cut of fear. Stupid, stupid! He should have known Vorhees would come looking for him. Should have been prepared for it.

Vorhees stomped past the wet bar and the long leather couch to the near corner of the desk. "I thought I'd find you here, Chaleen." Aggressive tone, hard-eyed stare — the bugger's pit bull mode.

"What's the idea busting in here like you

owned the place? It's after business hours
—"

"I didn't come on business. You know why I'm here."

"No, I don't. What do you want?" Chaleen was too rattled to keep a faint quaver out of his voice; hearing it made him angry, brought heat to his face. He had to will himself not to reach down for the glass of Glenlivet.

"What the fuck do you think? Cory Beckett."

"What about Cory Beckett?"

"Don't play dumb. And don't bother lying to me."

"I don't know what you're talking about."

"The hell you don't. I know you've been sleeping with her."

"Me? What gave you that idea?"

"She did. She admitted it to me."

"She wouldn't do that —"

Chaleen caught himself too late. Vorhees' lips peeled in against his teeth; he stomped forward until only a few inches separated them. "I knew it was true," he said. Spittle came out with the words, sprayed hot against Chaleen's face. "You sneaking, backbiting son of a bitch."

"It's not true. Listen to me, Andy —"

"Shut up! *You* do the listening." Vorhees

234

poked him in the chest with a forefinger. "It wasn't enough for you to cozy up with Margaret. No, you had to put the moves on Cory, too. Prove what a stud you are." Another poke, harder than the first. "How difficult was it to get into her pants? Easy? Or did you have to work at it?"

It was easy! I didn't put the moves on her, she put them on me! But he shook his head, didn't say anything.

"How long has it been going on? How long?"

"Back off, damn you."

"Answer me. How easy? How long?"

"No. Get out of here."

"Not until you tell me the truth, admit what a scumbag you are."

"I'm not going to admit anything to you."

"She's mine, Chaleen. You hear me?" Another jab, two fingers this time and hard enough to hurt. "She made a stupid mistake with you and she knows it. Now I want to hear you say you know it. Say 'She's yours, Andy, all yours.' Say 'I won't go near her from now on.' "

Anger swelled in Chaleen; he swatted the thrusting hand away. "And if I don't?"

"You will, by God, if you know what's good for you. 'She's yours, Andy, all yours.' Say it."

"No!"

"I'm not leaving until you do. Neither are you."

"You want me to call the cops? Trespassing on private property, making a lot of crazy accusations, threatening me —"

"What do you need the cops for? Why don't you go ahead and throw me out yourself?"

Chaleen could feel himself sweating. He had five years, ten pounds, and a couple of inches on Vorhees, but the bastard was in better shape, had done some boxing in college.

"I'm warning you —"

Vorhees laughed in his face. "Afraid to brawl with me? Sure you are. Just like that night at the Red Fox."

"That was a public place, this is my private office —"

"You didn't have the balls then, you don't have the balls now. You're a coward, Chaleen."

"Don't call me that."

"A sly, sneaky coward. Always have been, always will be."

"I'm not a coward!"

"Prove it. Come on, coward, show me I'm wrong, show me how much you hate my guts."

The anger was a roaring in Chaleen's head now, but it still wasn't hot enough to burn away the fear. He stood there flat-footed, sweating.

"All right then," Vorhees said, "I'll show you how much I hate yours."

When the jab came this time, it was with the heel of Vorhees' hand — a blow with enough force to drive Chaleen backward. His feet tangled together; he fell sideways into his desk chair, skidding it, then upending it so that when he caromed off onto the floor the chair clattered over on top of him. One of the padded arms slammed into his chin, jammed the back of his head and neck into the carpet.

A sunburst of pain swirled fear and anger together, dizzied his thoughts, distorted his hearing so that Vorhees' voice saying, "Get up, you're not hurt," seemed to come humming from a distance. It was his hands and fingers that reacted, without conscious will, as if they were independent entities: shoving the chair off, reaching upward to clutch and hang onto the edge of the desk and lift himself onto his feet.

" 'She's yours, Andy, all yours.' " Vorhees' voice was clearer now, the words arrogant, commanding. " 'I'll never go near her again.' "

Chaleen leaned shakily on the desktop. He heard himself say in a cracked voice, "Get away, get out."

" 'She's yours, Andy, all yours.' "

"Get out, get out!"

Through a haze of pain and sweat he saw Vorhees come toward him, felt a handful of his shirt caught and bunched and his body jerked close. "Say it, you piece of shit!"

Again it was the fingers of his right hand that reacted without conscious thought. Scrabbled forward, touched the coldness of the heavy rose quartz paperweight, gathered it into his palm —

"Say it!"

— and blindly, then, his arm swung up and swept around, and he heard the crunch of stone meeting flesh and bone, felt warm wet droplets spatter his face, felt the grip on his shirtfront release. His fingers went nerveless; the paperweight bounced, rolled on the desktop. Shock waves rolled through him. Clearly, then, he saw Vorhees still standing, a look of disbelief on his face, the extended hand fluttering as if with sudden palsy, a crimson and bone-white hole in his forehead where the left eyebrow had been.

"No," Chaleen said, "no, I didn't mean —"

Vorhees' eyes glazed over and he collapsed

into a loose bundle on the carpet.

Numbly, Chaleen stared down at him. It seemed like a long time before he could make his legs carry him forward. In what felt like slow-motion movements, he lowered himself to one knee beside Vorhees, fumbled for a pulse that wasn't there.

Dead.

Dead!

Nausea churned in his stomach, funneled bile into his throat. He lurched to his feet, stumbled around the couch into the bathroom, reached the toilet just as the scotch came boiling and burning out of him. He hung there, retching, until there was nothing left. At the sink then, not looking into the mirror before or after, he scrubbed the blood spatters off his face. His hands still shook badly when he was done; his breathing was erratic, he couldn't seem to get enough oxygen into his lungs.

In his office again, not looking at what lay on the carpet, he took two long pulls from the bottle of Glenlivet. The whiskey burned like fire, stayed down, but did little to quiet his screaming nerves or ease the feeling of suffocation. Unsteadily, he went through the front office, opened the outer door, stepped outside to suck in deep breaths of the cold night air —

Christ! Vorhees had left the gates standing wide open.

The thought that somebody, one of the homeless that hung around the area, might've come wandering in ran a shudder through Chaleen. No cars on the street now, nobody in sight, but he ran across the night-lit yard anyway, closed the gate, snapped the padlock. His chest heaved like a bellows on the way back.

Inside again, he locked the outer door. Sat down at Abby's desk to try to get his breathing under control, try to think.

What was he going to do?

Dead man in his office. Bastard deserved to die, but not like this, not here. The other night with Margaret had been bad enough, but all he'd had to do then was make sure she drank enough to pass out, then carry her out to the garage and fire up her Mercedes. No blood, no violence, no body to worry about. And he hadn't had to watch her die.

But it wasn't a detached murder this time, wasn't murder at all. Vorhees had hit him, knocked him down, grabbed him, threatened him . . . he'd acted in self-defense. Call the police? Tell them how Vorhees had bulled in here, but not the reason, and then the rest of it just as it had happened. They'd believe him. Wouldn't they?

Maybe they wouldn't. No marks on him to show that he'd been attacked; he felt his head and neck to be sure. Common knowledge that he and Vorhees had had trouble before. There'd be an investigation and the cops would find out about him and Cory from those two private dicks. And what if they got it in their heads to question Margaret's death despite the accident verdict, somehow managed to tie him to it? He wasn't sure he was in any shape to stand up to police questioning tonight, or at any time. Calling the law was out, it would only make things worse.

Get rid of the body. That was what he had to do. Take it somewhere and hide it, bury it, or at least make it look like Vorhees was killed someplace else by somebody else. But what about Vorhees' car? That damn Aston was parked right out front. He couldn't leave it there, and he couldn't drive two cars. Didn't dare run the risk of ditching the Aston after ditching the body and then taking a taxi or public transportation to come back for his Caddy —

Cory!

She'd know what to do, she'd help him.

Call her, explain what had happened, tell her —

Tell her he'd just killed her future husband, the man who was going to make her rich? Tell her all her carefully laid plans had been for nothing and both of them might be up shit creek now? She wouldn't care that it had been self-defense, she'd blame him for letting it happen. Never forgive him, never let him near her again. He'd lose her for good.

No, he *couldn't* ask her for help, couldn't ever tell her what had happened here tonight. Didn't make any difference whether Vorhees was found dead or just disappeared without a trace; either way, Chaleen's only hope of keeping her was to plead ignorance and make her believe it.

The body, the car . . . he'd have to get rid of them by himself. No other choice. But how?

Think, think!

He went back into his office for another jolt of Glenlivet. This one steadied him, helped him focus. And pretty soon an idea began to form. He clung to it, shaped it until it was complete. Or almost complete. There was still the problem of the two cars, getting back here to claim his own after he got rid of the body and Vorhees' Aston. . . .

One more drink, a small one this time, and he had the answer. George Petrie. Old George, factory foreman at Chaleen Manufacturing from the day the old man opened the plant. Loyal as they come. Do any favor he was asked to, even after business hours, and without asking questions of his own. And he was guaranteed reachable by phone; a widower, old George never went out on weeknights by his own admission.

Chaleen made himself go look at the body. The way Vorhees had fallen, half over on his left side, most of the blood from the wound glistened on his face and shirt and coat. Not much on the carpet, just a few spots. More spots on the desktop, smeared on the paperweight. The clean-up wouldn't be too bad. But he'd have to get that started first, before the blood dried. Then he'd get a tarp from the factory and roll the body into it before he carried it out to the Aston.

All right. Now that Chaleen had a plan in place he was steady-handed again, his control regained. When the salvage job was finished, there'd be nothing to tie Vorhees' death to him. He'd still have Cory, and before long they'd figure a way, or she would, to get their hands on the kind of money she coveted and he needed.

It could, it would work out that way. It *had* to!

22

Tamara and Runyon were discussing Andrew Vorhees' no-show when I came into the agency. Vorhees still seemed to be missing this morning; there'd been no word from him, and when Tamara called his office, she got the kind of tight-lipped runaround that indicates something amiss.

"Something's happened to him," she said ominously, "and you can bet Cory Beckett had a hand in it."

Jumping to conclusions as she often did, I thought at the time, but it turned out that on this occasion she was at least half right. Something *had* happened to Andrew Vorhees, the kind of something that would be overheated media fodder for days to come.

We had advance word before the news became public. Tamara had texted her Hall of Justice pipeline, a woman named Felicia who worked in the SFPD's computer section, asking for any information the Department might have on Vorhees. The answer she received prompted a furious series of back-and-forth texts to learn the details.

Vorhees was dead. Bludgeoned to death, the apparent victim of a carjacking. A patrol unit had spotted his Aston Martin speeding on Geneva Avenue near the Crocker Amazon Playground shortly after 2:00 A.M.; the driver, a nineteen-year-old youth from the projects, refused to stop and there'd been a brief high-speed chase that ended when the kid missed a turn and ran the Aston into a light pole. When the cops checked the trunk, they found Vorhees' body stuffed inside.

The ghetto youth and his passenger cousin admitted they'd stolen the car, but swore they hadn't committed the murder, hadn't had any idea there was a dead man in the trunk. Their story was that they'd seen the Aston parked on a street in Visitacion Valley, the keys in the ignition, and decided to take it for a ride. The police weren't buying. Both suspects had juvenile rap sheets for stealing and stripping cars, and though the murder weapon hadn't been found with the body, the assumption was that the youths had tossed it and were heading somewhere to get rid of the body when they were spotted.

"Crap," Tamara said. "Pure crap."

"You don't think it was a carjacking?" I asked her.

"No way."

I didn't think so, either, but I said, "Why not?"

"Bunch of reasons. Too big a coincidence, for one — Vorhees suddenly turning up dead so soon after his wife and just when he's getting ready to hire us."

"Go on."

"Carjackers and guys that jump iron off the streets are different breeds of cat. No 'jacking on these two kids' sheets."

"They're only nineteen. Maybe they decided to change their MO."

She made a face to indicate what she thought of that explanation. "You ever hear of a 'jacker whacking a car owner with some kind of round blunt instrument? Uh-uh. Guns or knives."

"Good point," Runyon said, and I agreed.

Tamara said, "Then there's the preliminary coroner's report. Felicia says Vorhees'd been dead for hours when the body was found, maybe as many as seven or eight. No streetwise kids are gonna waste somebody, hang onto the hot car *and* the corpse for seven or eight hours, and then go out speeding with it on a city street."

An even better point.

"So if it wasn't a 'jacking," she said, "and those dudes are telling the truth, why was Vorhees' expensive wheels on the street in Visitacion Valley with him dead in the trunk and the keys in the ignition? So it'd get stolen, right? So whoever swiped it would get stuck with the corpse, right?"

"Assume a setup, then," I said. "Who's responsible?"

"Cory Beckett, who else."

"All by herself? A woman who has a history of not dirtying her own hands?"

"I didn't say that."

"Who did the job, then? Frank Chaleen?"

"Sure. Got him to do Vorhees' wife, didn't she?"

"We don't know that for sure. If Margaret Vorhees' death was premeditated murder, then it was strictly for gain. Cory's whole focus is money and power; presumably that's why she took up with Vorhees in the first place. Why would she suddenly want him dead?"

"On account of he dumped her and she was pissed at losing her meal ticket."

"That's another thing we don't know for sure, that he dumped her," I pointed out.

"Confronted her about Chaleen, yes, but that's all."

Runyon agreed. "Seems to me her reaction if he tried to walk away would be the opposite of violence — use every trick she knows to get him back on the hook."

"Right. And if that didn't work, she'd just lick her wounds and start looking for another mark. Vorhees isn't the only wealthy yachtsman around who can be seduced and bled."

Tamara wanted Cory Beckett to be guilty of both homicides. She said stubbornly, "Her motive doesn't have to be revenge. Maybe offing him is what she was planning all along."

"Same objection," I said. "Nothing in it for her."

". . . Well, suppose Vorhees changed his will, put her in for a big slice of his estate? She'd want him dead before he could change it, right?"

"Now you're reaching. No matter how smitten Vorhees was with her, he'd have to be a fool to change his will in her favor while he was still married or immediately after his wife's death. Whatever else he was, he was no fool when it came to money. He'd have waited until he was married to Cory before he made her his heir, and then not until he was completely sure of her. Same reasoning if she wanted him dead: after they were married, not before."

Tamara scowled, but she didn't argue the point. "All right, then how about this? She found out somehow he was hiring us to investigate her and there's something heavy in her past she's afraid we'll find out."

"A skeleton she wants to keep closeted desperately enough to toss the rest of her plans and commit murder? Doesn't seem likely. Besides, you'd have already picked up a hint if there was."

"Not necessarily. I dug pretty deep, but I didn't hit bottom."

"Close to it, though. You can keep digging, but do you really believe you'll find those kind of buried bones?"

No, she didn't — I could see it in her expression — but she wouldn't admit it. And she still wasn't ready to let go of the subject. She said, "So maybe Cory didn't have anything to do with it. Maybe Chaleen did Vorhees on his own."

"For what reason?"

"So he could have her all to himself."

"Blow up her plans, do both of them out of a piece of Vorhees' money? That doesn't wash, either."

"He wouldn't dare cross her," Runyon

agreed. "She'd eat him alive."

"Okay, okay," Tamara said grumpily. "So it wasn't Cory and it wasn't Chaleen. But it wasn't any freakin' carjacker, either."

"Vorhees was the kind of man who made enemies," I said. She opened her mouth, but I held up a hand before she could say anything. "I know, I know. The long arm of coincidence again."

Runyon said, "SFPD'll find out who did it and why. High-profile victim, high-priority investigation."

"The kind that might just bring Cory and Chaleen down, whether or not they had anything to do with what happened last night."

"Believe it when I see it," Tamara said. Then she said, "Cops are bound to get around to us sooner or later. What do we tell them?"

"As much as we know to be fact," I said. "Nothing more, nothing that crosses legal and ethical lines."

"Otherwise we stay out of it."

"That's right. Even if Vorhees had signed a client's contract, we'd have to stay out of it. The police wouldn't give us permission for an independent investigation in a case like this."

Tamara sighed. "Stuck in neutral again.

Sometimes I wish we didn't always have to go by the book."

"We wouldn't stay in business long if we didn't."

As expected, the media — local and national both — milked Vorhees' murder for all it was worth. Statements from and interviews with the chief of police, union and City Hall officials; editorials on crime in the streets; rehash features on Vorhees' scandal-ridden personal life and the recent death of his wife. I didn't see or read any of the reportage; secondhand commentary from Tamara and Kerry was enough for me. I tend to avoid all direct contact with print and broadcast journalism, particularly where sensational crime news is concerned. Kerry says, only half kidding, that I'm an ostrich in the current events sandbox. Guilty.

Evidently the SFPD wasn't any more satisfied with the carjacking explanation than we were. Except for the usual stock handouts, they put a tight lid on their investigation. So tight that Tamara's friend Felicia refused all further requests for progress information.

The homicide inspectors in charge got around to us soon enough. They interviewed Tamara alone first on Thursday; Runyon and I weren't in the office at the time. They talked to me at home, and Jake at the Hall of Justice where he went voluntarily.

The three of us had worked out exactly what we would and wouldn't be free to say, and for once Tamara held herself in check and followed instructions. Runyon's private conversations with Kenneth Beckett were one of the off-limits topics; our suspicions that Margaret Vorhees' death was premeditated murder was another. This is what we admitted to:

That Runyon and I had spoken to Andrew Vorhees in his office the day before he was killed, at his request. That he'd wanted to know what we knew about his wife's death, which was nothing more than what Runyon had told the police after his discovery of Margaret Vorhees' body. That it was common knowledge Vorhees had been involved with a woman named Cory Beckett, who had at one time been our client, and her name had come up during the course of the conversation. That a former friend and campaign worker of his, Frank Chaleen, was reputed to also be having an affair with the Beckett woman, and that Vorhees had been upset about it. And that Vorhees had called in person the following day with the stated intention of hiring us, saying he would explain what he wanted us to do when he met with Runyon that evening on his yacht.

There was enough inference in all of this to put the inspectors onto the Cory Beckett cabal, if they weren't already headed in that direction and whether or not either she or Chaleen was involved in the Vorhees homicide. The two of them would tell different stories than we had, of course, but it was their word against ours and we were on pretty solid ground. For all we could tell, the closemouthed inspectors seemed to think so, too. There had not been a suspicious or adversarial edge to the interview with me, nor to the ones with Jake and Tamara.

That was the way things stood through Friday. No more visits from the police. No new information leaked to or revealed in the media. And no word from Cory Beckett, her brother, or Frank Chaleen.

On Saturday, Kerry and I had a small argument over her mother's cremains. It started when I suggested that it would be a good day, the weather being clear and sunny, for the three of us to drive over to Marin County and honor Cybil's wish to have her ashes scattered in Muir Woods.

"I don't think that's a good idea," she said.

"Why not? Too soon?" She'd gotten the box of cremains from the Larkspur mortuary on Wednesday.

"No, not exactly."

"What then, exactly?"

"I'm not so sure we ought to do it at all."

"Why not? It's what Cybil wanted."

"I know that, but . . . Muir Woods, a national park full of people on nice weekends."

"We can find a private place off one of the trails."

"Even so. You know as well as I do it's against the law to scatter human remains in a public place."

"A misdemeanor that a great many people don't happen to believe should be a crime at all. Loved ones' ashes are scattered in natural surroundings every day with no harm done."

She gave me one of her sidewise looks. "You've always been such a stickler for following the letter of the law," she said. "This bizarre business with Andrew Vorhees and the Becketts, for instance. And now you want to step over the line."

"A stickler professionally, yes, for the most part, especially when a case involves a couple of homicides and the integrity of the agency. But I freely admit to having bent and stretched points of law a few times, and even to committing a couple of small felonies when it seemed necessary."

"So you're honest and law-abiding only when it suits you."

I said gently, "Kerry, I'm going to make an observation. Think about it before you snap back at me."

"What observation?"

"That you're reluctant to scatter Cybil's ashes for the same reason you have her personal belongings displayed in your office and you're determined to get all her fiction back into print."

"What are you saying? I'm trying to keep her with me even though she's dead and gone?"

"Yes, and there's nothing wrong with that. Up to a point. But buying an urn for the ashes, putting it in your office with the rest of her stuff —"

"I wasn't going to do that."

"The box is in there now, isn't it? On the bookcase?"

She had no answer for that.

"I'm not criticizing you," I said, "and I'm not saying this to hurt you. I know how important it is for you to keep Cybil's memory alive; I'm in complete agreement there. But holding onto her cremains is not only borderline morbid, it goes against her express wishes and your promise to honor them. You never defied your mother when she was alive. Don't start now."

She moved away from me without answering, out onto the balcony where she stood stiffly outlined against the sweeping view of the city and the bay. I had the good sense not to follow her. She was not out there very long. And when she came back inside, it was without any trace of anger or resentment.

"I thought it over," she said, "and you're right. You know me so well it's scary sometimes."

"Not as well as you know me. Which is even scarier."

That earned me a wan smile. "You fetch Emily while I get ready. Then we'll head over to Marin."

We spent two hours in Muir Woods, part of it wandering the network of marked trails among the groves of giant coast redwoods in search of a suitable spot. When we found one, we slipped off among the towering trees — another small law respectfully broken — and once we were sure we were alone and unobserved, Kerry opened the mortuary container and carefully scattered Cybil's ashes among several of the tall trees.

Then the three of us held hands and murmured words of remembrance to one another and thought our private thoughts. Kerry was solemn throughout; I imagined she might cry a little, but she didn't. She gave me another small smile, this one sad, wistful, on the walk back to the car.

All in all, it was a private, peaceful, dignified ceremony.

We agreed that Cybil would have approved.

I treated Kerry and Emily to Sunday morning brunch, and afterward we went to the park for a leisurely walk around Stowe Lake, then home to our individual pursuits. Normal, quiet, relaxing day that I expected would continue through to bedtime.

But it didn't.

Because this was the day the Cory Beckett powder keg suddenly and lethally blew up.

23

JAKE RUNYON

Most wage earners look forward to time off on weekends, one or two days of freedom to rest, putter, engage in recreational pastimes. Runyon wasn't one of them anymore. Not after the long, empty months in Seattle following Coleen's slow and agonizing death, not after the move to San Francisco and his failure to end the long estrangement with Joshua, not even after he'd become involved with Bryn. Work was his primary focus, the one thing he was good at, the only activity that gave him any real satisfaction.

Weekends when he had no business to occupy his time were nothing more than a string of hours of enforced waiting, to be endured and gotten through. He had no hobbies, no particular interest in sports or cultural events; he was constitutionally incapable of sleeping more than five or six hours a night, or of sitting around the apartment reading or staring at the tube or just vegetating. An active diversion more job-related than pleasurable was the only sure way he'd found to deal with those empty Saturdays and Sundays: close himself inside the Ford and burn up long miles and tanksful of gas on the highways, back roads, streets, and byways of the greater Bay Area and beyond, familiarizing and refamiliarizing himself with the territory and what went on in each part of it. The better he knew his turf, the better he could do his job.

This weekend was not one of the empty ones. This Saturday and Sunday he'd been working a field case, acting on a hunch. It was one of the few jobs he disliked on general principle, involving stakeouts and spy photography, but he didn't mind it so much in this case because the subject was the sort of scofflaw it would feel good to take down.

The stakeout was in Belmont, near a fairly affluent tract home owned by a businessman in his forties named Garza. Garza had a large accident policy with Northwestern Insurance and had put in a claim citing an on-the-job injury that prevented him from doing any sort of manual labor. He had a doctor's report to back him up. Northwestern smelled fraud and hired the agency to investigate, with Runyon being given the assignment.

Fraud was what it was. He'd found out that Garza and the doctor were old high school buddies who played golf together now and then, conducted a couple of drive-bys at Garza's home and business, and finally readied his digital camcorder and began the stakeouts in the hope of proving the subject wasn't anywhere near as incapacitated as he claimed.

The Saturday stakeout had been a bust; Garza had spent most of the day at the small plumbing supply company he owned, supervising his handful of employees and doing nothing contrary to his injury claim. The hunch that had drawn Runyon to the subject's house today was the fact that Garza was having a new driveway put in. The man was too smart to do any heavy work at his place of business, but there was the chance that he'd decided to cut costs by doing some of the driveway renovation himself.

Most of the day it had looked like another bust. But then a little past three-thirty, Garza figured it was safe enough to put in a couple of hours of work on the driveway.

The garage door went up and there he was, coming out with a shovel in hand. He looked around without spotting Runyon in the Ford, then started shoveling and spreading gravel. No strain, no pain, not even a wince while he worked.

Runyon had recorded three full minutes of damning video when his cell vibrated. He put the camcorder down before he checked the phone. And then he forgot all about Garza.

The caller was Kenneth Beckett, with his third and final cry for help.

"Help me, Mr. Runyon. Please. I don't want to do it."

The naked desperation in the kid's voice put Runyon on instant alert. He could feel himself going tight inside and out. "I don't understand. What don't you want to do?"

"The gun . . . I couldn't, I couldn't . . ."

"Cory's gun?"

"She said I had to do it because of what happened to Mr. Vorhees." The kid's shaky voice changed, rose in the falsetto imitation of his sister's. " 'He's out of control, Kenny, we can't let him hurt us, too.' "

Chaleen. Vorhees' killer after all, for some reason as yet unclear. And Cory found out about it. And now, in her warped mind, it was payback time.

"But it's not right," Beckett said. "Even a bastard like him, even if he did what she said . . . it's not right. I tried to do it like she told me to but I *can't.*"

"Then don't. Don't! You understand me?"

A kind of moan and then silence.

"Ken? Where are you calling from?"

"His place. She let me have my cell, so I could call her when it's over, but I . . ."

"You haven't called her?"

"No, I couldn't. Just you."

"Chaleen's place, you said. His home?"

"He's in there. Cory put something in his drink when they were together before. He . . ." The falsetto again. " 'It'll be easy, all you have to do is put the gun to his head and close your eyes and squeeze the trigger. . . .' "

"Ken, listen to me. Chaleen's home, is that where you're at?"

". . . No. The factory."

"And you're where now, exactly? Inside? Outside?"

"In my van, out front."

"All right. Stay there. Don't leave the van, don't call Cory, don't do anything. I'll be there as soon as I can. You understand?"

Runyon was talking to himself. The line hummed emptily.

■ ■ ■ ■

It took him twenty-five minutes of fast driving to cover the distance from Belmont to Chaleen Manufacturing in the city. Nearing dusk by the time he reached Basin Street. The industrial area was quiet, Sunday deserted. When Runyon entered the last block, drove past the factory grounds, the ropy muscles in his shoulders and back drew even more taut.

The street was empty of vehicles of any kind, and the only one inside the chain-link fence, parked in the shadows next to the detached office building, was a newish black Cadillac. There was no sign of the blue Dodge van.

The kid hadn't waited.

Drawn back to the flame again.

Runyon braked in front of the closed office gates. Before he got out he unlocked the glove compartment, removed the .357 Magnum from its chamois wrapping, holstered it, and clipped the holster to his belt.

A chill bay wind played with scraps of litter, swirling them along the uneven pavement, forming little heaps against the bottom of the fence; a fast-food bag slapped his leg as he stepped up to the gates. The two halves were drawn together, but not locked: a big Yale used to padlock them hung by its staple from one of the links. He pushed through, his steps echoing hollowly on the uneven pavement.

Somebody had torn the WE'RE ECO-FRIENDLY! poster off the office door; one corner of it was all that was left, the loose piece flapping in the wind. The doorknob turned freely under Runyon's hand. He pushed the door inward, looked into the outer office without entering. Lighted, but empty.

He called Chaleen's name. No answer.

Once more, shouting it this time. Still no answer.

He went in then, leaving the door standing open behind him, one hand on the Magnum. The two inner doors were closed. The one on the far left would lead to a bathroom or storage room. He cracked the one in the middle. The large room beyond was also lighted. He called out again, heard nothing but the faint after-echo of his own voice, then widened the crack so he had a clear look inside.

Chaleen's private office, large enough to take up most of the back half of the building. Desk, chairs, wet bar, couch, a shaded lamp on the desk supplying the light.

And Frank Chaleen sitting in a sideways sprawl on the couch, head flung back, eyes shut, one arm dangling.

At first Runyon thought he was dead. But there was no blood or other signs of violence on Chaleen or the cushions under him, and as Runyon moved closer he could hear the faint rasp of the man's breathing. Passed out drunk was the way it looked; you could detect the odor of liquor on his breath, and on a table next to the couch was a nearly empty glass of what smelled like expensive scotch.

But the way it looked wasn't the way it was.

Runyon used a thumb to raise one closed eyelid. Drugged; the size of the pupil confirmed it. Beckett, on the phone: *Cory put something in his drink when they were together before.* Together here? No, she wouldn't have run that risk. Probably arranged to meet Chaleen in a bar or restaurant not too far away, spiked his drink with something slow-acting like benzodiazepine, then sent him here on some pretext with a promise to meet him later. The drink he'd poured for himself from his wet bar would have helped deepen the drug's effect when it finally took hold.

And once he was unconscious, Beckett

was supposed to come in and finish the job. Shoot Chaleen point-blank in the head, make it look like suicide. Another reprise of Cory's cold, evil MO: leave the dirty work, the wet work, to the men in her life, and her brother was the only one left. Except that she'd overestimated her power to manipulate Kenneth into an act he was incapable of committing. But he must have come close because he'd been in here with the gun and something else Cory had given him, the sheet of bond paper that now lay crumpled on the floor in front of the couch.

Runyon picked up the paper, smoothed it out. Chaleen Manufacturing letterhead stationery with six lines of computer typing on it and Chaleen's scrawled signature at the bottom. But he hadn't typed it and he hadn't been the one to sign it.

I can't go on living. Business on the edge of bankruptcy, my whole life in shambles. I killed Andrew Vorhees. We had a fight and I hit him with a paperweight and put the body in his car and made it look like a carjacking. The police are suspicious, they'll find out, I can't face prison. This is the best way for everybody.

The hell it was. Best for Cory. Only Cory.

Runyon shoved the phony suicide note into his pocket, then made a quick search under and around the couch and of the rest of the office. There was no sign of Cory's small-caliber automatic; Beckett had taken it with him.

At the door Runyon cast one more look at Chaleen. Limbs starting to twitch a little now; pretty soon he'd wake up sick and bewildered. But not half as sick as he'd be when he took the fall for killing Vorhees.

Runyon was in the Ford and on his way down Basin Street before he rang Bill's home number. Caught him in, gave him a terse report — what Beckett had told him, what he'd found in Chaleen's office, what he was afraid might happen or have already happened.

Bill said, "The kid may not have gone back to the apartment. If he's enough afraid of his sister . . ."

"Plenty afraid, but he won't be able to stay away from her. He's like a whipped dog with nowhere else to go."

"She wouldn't hurt him. It's not her style."

"Not normally, but she's bound to be furious when he tells her he didn't go through with it. I'm on my way there now."

"Intervention? Cory could make a lot of trouble if he refuses to give her up."

"I know it, but I don't see any other choice now — I've got to try for his sake. I'll take full responsibility —"

"No, you won't," Bill said. "I'll meet you there and we'll see this through together."

24

I had a shorter distance to travel, so I got to the Nob Hill address ahead of Runyon. The blue Dodge van wasn't anywhere in the immediate vicinity, but that didn't mean anything. The neighborhood has a smattering of small parking garages where residents pay outlandish monthly fees to lodge their vehicles. I left my car in the nearest one, the hell with the expense.

While I waited I paced the sidewalk in front, looking up at the lighted windows of the Beckett apartment. No telling for sure if both of them were in there; the curtains were closed. I wondered if Runyon and I were going to have trouble getting in, first to the building and then to the apartment. We couldn't go barreling through doors like a couple of commandos; admittance, at least to the building, had to be by permission.

If we did get into the apartment and Beckett was all right, I was not looking forward to the face-off with Cory. We had plenty of circumstantial ammunition against her, but none of it, including the fake suicide note, was much good from a legal standpoint unless we could convince the kid to open up to the authorities. If he sided with his sister, let her control him and the situation, we'd have no choice but to back off again.

I'd been there ten minutes when Runyon came hurrying up the block. We conferred in the foyer while he leaned on the bell. I expected it to be a while before we got a response, if we got one, and that the first thing we'd hear then was a voice on the intercom. But it was only a few seconds before the door buzzer went off, while the intercom stayed silent.

Neither Jake nor I said anything on the way inside. I could feel a sharpening tension. Nothing either of the Becketts did was completely predictable, it seemed.

The door to their apartment stood ajar. That ratchetted the tension up another notch. The sudden constricted feeling in my gut was one I'd had before, a sixth-sense warning sign: *something wrong here.* From the look on Runyon's face, he felt it, too. He was armed as a precaution; he'd mentioned it in the foyer. I saw him put a hand on the holstered Magnum under his coat and keep it there as we moved ahead to the door.

We went in slow and cautious, Jake announcing us on the way. Almost immediately Kenneth Beckett answered in a flat, toneless voice, "In here, Mr. Runyon."

So he was all right. One hurdle cleared.

Beckett was in the gaudily decorated living room, sitting stone-rigid on a chair in front of one of the gold-flecked mirrors, fingers splayed like hooks over his knees. Alone in there, his sister nowhere in sight. His unblinking gaze shifted from Runyon to me and then fastened on Jake. If Beckett saw me at all, he didn't care who I was or why I was there. The look of his eyes — dark, opaque, like burned-out bulbs — confirmed my gut feeling of wrongness. So did a pair of long, fresh scratches below his left cheekbone, the blood from them still oozing a little.

Runyon said to him, "Why didn't you wait for me at the factory, Ken?"

"Cory."

"You called her after we talked? Or did she call you?"

"She did."

"Did you tell her you'd talked to me, that I was on my way there?"

"No."

"But you told her you couldn't do what she wanted."

"She said if I didn't, she didn't want anything more to do with me. . . . I wasn't her brother anymore. But I couldn't go back in there. I thought if I could just make her understand. . . ." He shook his head, a wobbly, broken movement. "Cory," he said then. And again, twice, like a half-whispered lament, "Cory. Cory."

"Where is she?"

"I'm sorry. Oh God, Cory, I'm sorry!"

"Where, Ken?"

Nothing for several seconds. Then Beckett lifted one hand in a vague gesture toward the rear of the apartment, let it fall back bonelessly onto his lap. Closed his eyes and sat there mute.

I moved first, with Runyon close on my heels. The kitchen and dining rooms were empty. So was the first bedroom, hers, that opened off a central hallway. The adjacent bathroom was where we found her — a luxury bathroom with gold-rimmed mirrors set into baby-blue tile, a sunken tub, and a glass-block shower stall. The air in there was moist, as if a bath or shower had been taken not long before, and thick with the odors of soap and lotions.

And bodily waste.

And blood.

I smelled the waste as soon as I entered the bedroom, in time to gird myself before Runyon and I crossed over far enough to see the body. She lay sprawled on her back on a fuzzy black rug in front of the shower stall, a bright yellow robe covering her from neck to ankles. Alive, she'd been beautiful; dead, she was a torn, soiled, ugly travesty. The bullet had gone in under her chin at an upward angle, ripped through the side of her face and opened up her head above the temple. The stall door and glass blocks were streaked and spattered with blood, bone splinters, brain matter, the blood still wet and glistening. Dead less than half an hour.

Runyon said between his teeth, "God-damn it, *why* didn't he stay at the factory?"

There was nothing to say to that. My stomach was kicking like crazy; I'd seen dead bodies before, the bloody, twisted aftermath of violence in too many forms, but I had never become inured to the sight. The reaction was always the same: sickness and disgust mingled with sadness and an impotent anger at the inhumanity of it.

The gun was on the floor next to the body, a short-barreled .25 with pearl grips. Neither Runyon nor I touched it. We backed out of there, returned to the living room.

Kenneth Beckett was still sitting in the same rigid posture, but his face was no longer impassive. Muscles rippled beneath the skin, making his features shift and change shape like images in a kaleidoscope. Tears leaked now from the burned-out eyes, mixing with the blood from the scratches to form a reddish serpent line on one cheek. Soundless weeping.

Runyon went to him, said his name twice to get his attention. "Did you call the police?"

"No. I couldn't. I thought you'd come, so I just . . . waited."

My cue to make the 911 call. But even as I spoke to the police dispatcher, I watched the two of them and I could hear what they were saying to each other, Beckett responding in that same hollow voice.

"What happened, Ken?"

"I killed her."

"Not deliberately. You wouldn't do that."

"No. Never. Never."

"Tell me what happened."

It was a few seconds before Beckett answered. Then, in an agonized whisper, "So pissed at me because I didn't shoot Chaleen. Madder than I ever saw her before. She wouldn't listen, just kept screaming that

I betrayed her. 'Give me the gun,' she said, 'I'll go do it myself.' I . . . I didn't want to. She hit me, scratched me. That damn gun. She yanked it out of my pocket. I tried to take it back and . . . I don't know, it went off and she . . . she . . ."

His eyes squeezed shut, then popped wide open like eyes in a Keane painting. He made a low animal-like noise in his throat; swallowed to shut it off, and stumbled on. "I killed her. I loved her and I killed her. I wish I was dead, too. The gun . . . I put it under my chin and I tried . . . I tried, but I couldn't make myself do that, either."

Death wish already granted, I thought as I put down the phone and moved over to where they were. In a very real sense he'd died, too, the instant the bullet tore the life out of his sister.

"It was an accident, Ken," Runyon said. "It's not your fault, it's hers."

"No. Mine, and that stupid pig Chaleen's. That's what she called him. 'Stupid pig deserves to die.' Then why did she let him fuck her all that time? Mr. Vorhees, sure, but why *him*?"

Because she needed the kind of man he was, I thought. Read his character correctly, with that innate sense some corrupt individuals have for spotting one of their own, and knew he could be maneuvered into committing murder for her. But he would not have lasted long even if he hadn't been responsible for Andrew Vorhees' death; she'd have found a way to jettison him sooner or later. That could be the reason she'd bought the automatic.

"I tried to tell her I couldn't do it," Beckett was saying. "She wouldn't take no for an answer. She never took no for an answer. I loved her so much, I always did what she wanted me to. In the light or in the dark. But not that. Why didn't she understand, not something like that?"

Runyon said, "What do you mean, in the dark?"

"At night. In bed together."

"So you were sleeping with her."

No response for three or four beats. Then, "It wasn't wrong. She said so the first night she came into my room. It wasn't wrong because we loved each other."

"How old were you that first night?"

"Fifteen."

The queasy feeling in my stomach was stronger now. Runyon's expression said he'd had intimations of this just as I had. Held out hope that it wasn't so, just as I had — the reason neither of us had brought up the possibility in open conversation. The kind of woman Cory Beckett had been, the screwed-up mess Kenneth was. Sex had been her primary weapon, always, and she'd wielded it mercilessly with all kinds of men. But sweet Jesus, her own brother!

"But I wasn't enough for her," Beckett said. "She had to have all those others. I didn't mind so much until Hutchinson. It . . . it wasn't the same with her after him. Because she wasn't the same."

Hutchinson. The biker felon she'd taken up with in Riverside, the one who'd been shot and killed by police.

"He talked her into it. She said it was her idea, but it couldn't have been. He made her do it."

"Do what?" Runyon asked him.

"I hated looking at her after that. But I couldn't stop doing it to her, she wouldn't let me stop."

"Ken. What did Hutchinson make her do?"

"But only in the dark. Only in the dark. I couldn't stand seeing her the way she was in the light. That's why I covered her in the bathroom after I killed her. I . . . couldn't . . . stand . . ."

Runyon asked the question again, but Beckett was no longer listening. His facial muscles quit jumping and twitching, his tear-stained features smoothed out so that he looked about the age he'd been when his sister seduced him — a battered, crippled, very old fifteen. He sat staring sightlessly, his mouth moving but no words coming out. Lost now somewhere deep inside himself. Lost, probably, for as long as there was breath left in his body.

But Jake and I could not just stand there and wait for the police. I wish we had. It would have been better for both of us if we hadn't let Beckett's last words send us back into that bloody bathroom.

We stood looking down at what was left of Cory Beckett. One fold of the yellow robe, I noticed then, had been draped over the other, the belt untied. I could not quite bring myself to reach down and open the robe. It was Runyon, after a few seconds, who did that.

It takes a lot to shock men who have been in law enforcement as long as we have. Beckett's incest revelation had rocked us some, but what we saw revealed now, the reason why Cory had always worn clothing that covered her to the neck, was like a body blow. Runyon was not given to emotional outbursts; his whispered "Christ!" was a measure of how affected he was. All I could do was stand there gaping in silence.

279

Cory Beckett, femme fatale. The incestuous relationship with her brother was one of the new and terrible twists she'd brought to the role. This was the other, and in a way it was worse, much worse.

She was tattooed.

One single massive tattoo, the entire front of her torso used as a canvas to portray a scene out of Dante's Inferno.

In intricate detail the upthrust breasts had been turned into a pair of erupting volcanoes, the nipples so violently colored they resembled volcanic cores. And spilling down over both globes, down over her belly to meet at her shaved pubis and disappear into the hollow between her legs, was a trail of molten fire.

It was the kind of voluntary sexual mutilation that could drive some men wild with lust, make them easier to manipulate and control.

And easier to destroy.

ABOUT THE AUTHOR

Bill Pronzini has been nominated for, or won, every prize offered to crime fiction writers, including the 2008 Grand Master Award from the Mystery Writers of America. It is no wonder, then, that *Detroit Free Press* said of him, "It's always nice to see masters at work. Pronzini's clear style seamlessly weaves [storylines] together, turning them into a quick, compelling read." He lives and writes in California, with his wife, the crime novelist Marcia Muller. He is the author of *Vixen, Strangers, Nemesis* and many more.

The employees of Thorndike Press hope you have enjoyed this Large Print book. All our Thorndike, Wheeler, and Kennebec Large Print titles are designed for easy reading, and all our books are made to last. Other Thorndike Press Large Print books are available at your library, through selected bookstores, or directly from us.

For information about titles, please call:
  (800) 223-1244

or visit our Web site at:
  http://gale.cengage.com/thorndike

To share your comments, please write:
  Publisher
  Thorndike Press
  10 Water St., Suite 310
  Waterville, ME 04901